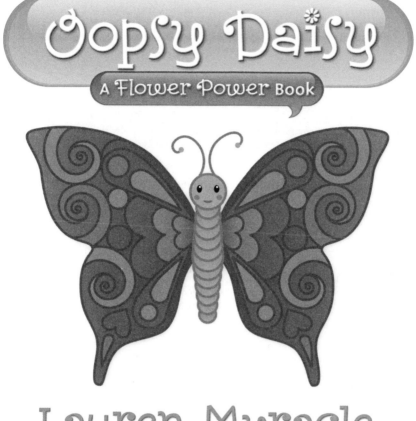

Oopsy Daisy

A Flower Power Book

Lauren Myracle

Amulet Books · New York

Cataloging-in-Publication Data has been applied for and may be obtained from the Library of Congress.
ISBN: 978-1-4197-0019-4

The text in this book is set in 11-point The Serif Light. The display typefaces are Annabelle, Chalet, FMRustlingBranches, RetrofitLight, Shag, and TriplexSans.

Text copyright © 2012 Lauren Myracle
Illustrations copyright © 2009–12 Christine Norrie
Book design by Maria T. Middleton

Printed and bound in U.S.A.
10 9 8 7 6 5 4 3 2 1

Amulet Books are available at special discounts when purchased in quantity for premiums and promotions as well as fundraising or educational use. Special editions can also be created to specification. For details, contact specialsales@abramsbooks.com or the address below.

ABRAMS
THE ART OF BOOKS SINCE 1949

115 West 18th Street
New York, NY 10011
www.abramsbooks.com

For
Elizabeth,
Lena,
and **Emma**,
whose mamacitas enrich y'all's lives
as well as mine

Sunday, October 16

The*rose*Knows

yes, my ever-adoring fans, it is I, Katie-Rose the

Magnificent, here to bring you this EXTREMELY IMPORTANT

public service announcement!

 The*rose*Knows

nods formally to Yasaman

The*rose*Knows

and thank you very muchly, Yazzikins, for making this

sparkly new LuvYaBunches.com page for us. yay! so now

whenever we have something EXTREMELY IMPORTANT to

say, we can say it to everyone all at once.

The*rose*Knows

onto my point—or, should I say, my big begonia!

The*rose*Knows

or begonias, plural, cuz I actually have 3 things to say.

The*rose*Knows

 #1: I made origami balloons today! the kind u blow air into

and they puff up? it took 4-evah to get it right, but I have now

mastered the skill, and I am vair vair proud of myself.

#2: I tried to turn them into origami water balloons, but

. . . no go. pulp city. they were still fun to throw, especially at Max. yes, Milla, I threw pulpy water blobs at yr boyfriend! nyah-nyah! 😊 it was pretty much yr fault, cuz the only reason Max came over was to ask if u were going to be at the Lock-In this Friday. I was like, "Max, u already know she is, so why r u asking?" he turned red and said, "I, uh, just . . . uh . . . wanted to make sure." which was, uh, malarkey, uh, so *I* said, "listen, bucko. u were my neighbor before u became milla's boyfriend, so don't u come to my house just so u can say her name. behavior like that is MUSHY and WRONG and AN EMBARRASSMENT TO YOUR SPECIES." then I pelted him with the water blobs. it was awesome.

🐶 #3: and this is THE BIG ONE! the BIGGEST of all the big begonias! VIOLET, WE ARE ALL SOOOOOOOOOOOOOO—big breath—OOOOOOOOO HAPPY YR MOM IS FINALLY HOME FROM THE HOSPITAL!!!! we can't wait to meet her, and we can't wait to hear how the homecoming went and all that. since yr not answering yr phone, and yr not online, I guess ur having family time, which I suppose is understandable. I mean, OF COURSE it's understandable.

×

The*rose*Knows

but like I said, we can't wait to meet her, and we even have a pressie for her. it's a welcome home gift, and technically Milla's moms bought it, but Milla said it can be from all of us. (thank u, Milla! and plz thank yr Mom Abigail and Mom Joyce for us!)

 The*rose*Knows

and now I will bid my fond farewell.

The*rose*Knows

blows smoochies

The*rose*Knows

till the morrow, my besties! and remember: we only have Monday, Tuesday, Wednesday, Thursday, and Friday (aren't u so proud of me for knowing the days of the week?) before . . . dum da-da dum . . . THE LOCK-IN on Friday night! *throws confetti* *throws begonias* *throws . . . uh . . . paper water balloons!*

 The*rose*Knows

BYE-ZEEZE!!!!

Monday, October 17

One

Camilla

Milla gets to school early, excited to see Violet. Her arms are wrapped around a potted plant, and she waddles down the hall because it's so big and she's so small. She's only small on the outside, though. Well, sometimes she feels small on the inside, but not today. Today, Milla is in a great mood. Today, goodwill radiates out of her and into the world, making her feel as if she and the world are one, and not for the first time she understands why the Bible says it's better to give than to receive.

It has nothing to do with sacrifice or doing the right thing or any of the reasons people often trot out when they want you to "be a good girl." In fact, Milla thinks that gift giving, when done right, is *totally* selfish, but in a good way. Giving is better than receiving because it makes your heart glow—and when that happens, everyone involved is sprinkled with happy dust, the gift-givers *and* the gift-getters.

She's eager to put this particular gift down, however. The terra cotta pot is heavy, and the leaves of the plant tickle her face. As she rounds a corner, she runs smack-dab into someone—*oomph*—and she reels backward.

"Omigosh, I am *so* sorry," she says, giggling despite her mortification. She rests the pot on her hip so she can issue a proper, face-to-face apology, but the plant is so lush that it takes Milla a moment to identify the girl she collided with. When she does, her words die in her throat. So do her giggles.

The girl, whose name is Modessa, snorts. She's beautiful on the outside, with shiny, flip-about hair and piercing blue eyes, but on the inside, she's as ugly as they come.

She's Milla's archenemy, and though Milla wishes she wasn't scared of her, she is.

"You're right, you *are* sorry," Modessa says.

A second girl laughs. "*Hunhhh. Good one.*"

Milla doesn't have a clear view of the second girl— too much potted plant, not enough space between its leaves—but she would know that phlegmy voice if she heard it oozing from a sewage pipe. It's Quin, Modessa's second-in-command.

"Yes, ha ha, very funny," Milla says, feeling her enthusiasm slip away like beads sliding from a broken necklace. She knows Modessa will do her best to humiliate Milla. She knows this because in a different lifetime—or what seems like a different lifetime—Milla and Modessa were friends. Quin, too.

Not all that long ago, they were a threesome: Modessa, Milla, and Quin. Only it wasn't a threesome like the Three Musketeers—all for one and one for all. It was all for Modessa, with Quin and Milla doing everything to please her, because if you didn't please Modessa, she made you pay. Just like she was going to make Milla pay now.

"So, *Camilla*," Modessa says, stretching Milla's full name out. Milla hates the way she does that. The way she savors it, as if it's hers to do with as she pleases. "I only ask because I'm curious"—loaded pause, enhanced by a snicker from Quin—"but . . . did you just ram me with a potted plant?"

"I said I'm sorry," Milla says. "Can you let me pass? Please?"

"Hmm," Modessa muses. "What do you think, girls? Should we?"

Girls, plural? How *many* girls? Milla twists awkwardly and glimpses a snatch of a pink plaid shirt through the leaves of the plant. There's a third girl there, all right, but Milla can't make out who it is.

Her muscles slump. She's surrounded, and other than their small group, there's no one else in the hallway.

"Not unless she passes a test," Quin says. "We should only let her by if she answers, like, a question, and it has to be a *hard* question."

Modessa makes a noncommittal sound, then addresses the third girl. The mystery girl. "What do you think? Should Milla have to pass a test?"

There's a tense sort of silence, followed by a thud. It could be flesh against flesh . . . or shoe against shin?

"Ow!" cries the mystery girl. "*Yes*. Yes, she should have to pass a test." The mystery girl swallows loudly. "Um, sorry, Milla."

Who is this girl who seems to be Modessa's new toy? Milla shuffle-steps in a circle, trying to get a better look at her. Pink plaid blouse: check. White jeans: check. On the girl's feet, pink cowboy boots—or cow*girl* boots, Milla supposes. It's a surprising touch, those pink boots. The sight of them makes Milla's brain go *ping! ping!* But she's unable to translate the *pings* into an actual recollection.

"*You* have no reason to say sorry," Modessa informs the mystery girl in pink boots. "*Camilla* rammed *me*. Remember? Camilla should say sorry."

And I did, Milla thinks, not that what's true and what's not has ever mattered to Modessa.

"I didn't see you," Milla says, keeping her voice as level as possible.

Modessa laughs. "You're so clumsy, Camilla. You always have been. Remember last summer, when we were at the pool? And you tripped on, like, a *Skittle*, and went flying into the lifeguard stand?"

Quin snickers. "And your top fell off, and the lifeguard was like, 'Why is this girl taking her bikini off in front of me?' Omigod. Hi*lar*ious."

It wasn't hilarious, and it wasn't a Skittle she tripped on. It was Quin's foot, which appeared out of nowhere at just the right time. No, at just the *wrong* time. And her bikini top did *not* fall off. It did need readjusting, however.

The memory of her humiliation hits her like a wave, causing her cells to tighten and draw in until she feels as if she's half her former size. Her body knows the sensation all too well, and not just from that day at the pool, but from a multitude of "good" times with Modessa.

Like in third grade, when Modessa told the whole class that Milla had diarrhea. Or in fourth grade, when Modessa wrote a mean poem about a teacher Milla liked, signed Milla's name to it, and left it on the teacher's desk, knowing Milla wouldn't have the guts to correct the misunderstanding.

Modessa justified her "jokes" by pretending they were part of a Milla improvement plan. "I'm *on your side*, Camilla. It's just, like, you have such low self-esteem."

Milla *does* have a problem with that. With self-esteem. She had hoped she was doing better, but apparently not if Modessa can still turn her into the amazing shrinking girl with one rude comment.

Standing in the hall, her biceps straining at the weight of the plant and her cheeks so hot that it feels as if her blood is trying to push its way out of her, Milla travels back in time.

Yesterday during Sunday School, the teacher passed out paper and crayons and told everyone to draw a picture of God's love. She said they could draw whatever they wanted, so Milla drew a picture of Katie-Rose, Yasaman, Violet, and herself—the flower friends—because if friendship wasn't love, she didn't know what was.

"Right on," the teacher said, kneeling by Milla. She pointed to the yellow-haired girl in the foursome. "Is this you?"

"Um, yeah?" Milla said.

The teacher laughed, and Milla didn't know why until her teacher said, "Oh, you sweet thing. Let me guess: You're the shortest girl in your class?"

"No," Milla said.

"I was, too, when I was your age," her teacher went on obliviously. "Kids would call me 'shrimp,' which I hated. My mother suggested I respond with, 'Yes, whale?' but I was like, 'Uh, no thanks, Mom. Great idea, but no.'"

Milla frowned, trying to figure out what she'd missed. She *wasn't* the shortest girl in her fifth-grade class. She wasn't the shortest of her flower friends, either. In terms of tallness, first came Violet, then Milla, then Yasaman, and, last of all, Katie-Rose. Katie-Rose was so short and teensy that people sometimes mistook her for a third grader, which drove Katie-Rose crazy.

Her Sunday School teacher moved on to admire someone else's work, and Milla studied her drawing. She'd drawn four girls jumbled up in a hug. So far, so good. But, wait. The blond girl in the picture—the one meant to be her—*was* shorter than the others. A full head shorter, and what was up with that?

Chills had tickled the back of her neck. It was true that

she wasn't the greatest artist, but she'd done the best she could. The Milla she sketched was wearing the same cute sweater dress as the real Milla, the same silver flats, and the same sparkly green scarf, which Mom Joyce had given her at the beginning of the school year and which Milla adored.

She got all of those details right, so why did she make herself so short? Shorter than Katie-Rose, even???

"Hey," Modessa says, snapping her fingers in the direction of Milla's face. "You could at least answer my question."

Question? Milla thinks. With an effort, she pulls herself back to the present. Does this have to do with the "test" they talked about giving her?

"Wh-what?" she says.

"Not answering someone's question is just *rude*. Right, Elena?"

Elena? The mystery girl is *Elena?!* Milla goes on a rapid-fire roller coaster ride, all inside her own head.

The pink cowboy boots. Duh. Elena lives on a farm. Milla has seen Elena wearing those boots before. She just didn't put the pieces together.

Why?

Because Elena is nice. The kind of girl who hand-makes cards for everyone on Valentine's Day. What in the world is she doing with Modessa and Quin?

Milla's emotions flip-flop. She hates that she still lets Modessa make her feel small, but now she's equally concerned—maybe *more* concerned—about Elena. What are Modessa and Quin up to? Why is Elena with them, going along with their mean Modessa-and-Quin games? What have the three of them been saying while she's been lost in her daze?

"Ask her again," Modessa says wearily. "Just ask the question again, and Camilla, just answer. God. Is it really so complicated?"

"Modessa wants to know if that plant thing is for your boyfriend," Quin says. "So is it?"

Milla tiny-steps farther around, and finally she can see all three girls clearly. They're stretched across the hall. "No, it's not for my boyfriend, and would you move, please?"

"Is it for Mr. Emerson?" Quin says. She makes kissy sounds. "Are you his wittle-bitty teacher's pet?"

Milla looks at Elena, whose pretty eyes are wider than Milla has ever seen them. *What's going on?* she asks Elena telepathically. *Are you trapped? Do you need help?*

Elena blinks several times.

Seeing Elena's fear calms Milla. She straightens her spine. "It's none of your business who it's for," she says. "But I'm about to drop it. Elena, want to help me carry it to my homeroom?"

Elena opens her mouth. "Uh . . . uh . . ." Her gaze goes to Modessa, then to Quin. She is a bobblehead doll whose head moves side-to-side instead of up and down.

Modessa pretends to hold back a laugh. She links her arm through Elena's and adopts a sickly-sweet tone. "Oh, sweetie, I don't think so," she says to Milla. "Favors are for friends, and no offense, but we don't really fall into that category, do we?"

"I'm not asking you. I'm asking Elena."

"Give it up, Milla," Modessa says, and her use of Milla's nickname, after making such a point to call her by her full name, is *not* a sign of goodwill. It's like Modessa is reminding her of what once was, when Milla was the girl Modessa linked arms with.

Modessa brushes past Milla, dragging Elena and Quin behind her. Milla is still worried about Elena, but stronger than her worry is her relief.

They're gone.

They're gone, and she *isn't* one of Modessa's friends/slaves/wannabes.

With a shudder, she pushes aside the whole yucky encounter, and now it's gone, too.

She tells herself it's gone, anyway. She tries to *make* it be gone.

When she reaches her classroom, she thunks the pot on her desk. *Phew*, her arms feel better. They're shaky, and she tells herself it's because of the weight of the pot. She rotates her wrists, lets out a big breath, and sits down. No one else has arrived yet, including Violet. But that's okay. She needs a few moments to process what she just went through.

She and Violet are both in Mr. Emerson's class, while Yasaman and Katie-Rose are in Rivendell's other fifth-grade class, with Ms. Perez. Ms. Perez is also Modessa and Quin's teacher. Ms. Perez is also Elena's teacher.

So that's how they got to her, Milla thinks, the "they" being Modessa and Quin, and the "her" being Elena. She imagines Modessa wooing Elena with compliments paired with insults, as that's Modessa's style. As in, "I *love* your boots. Most girls would look so babyish in pink cowboy boots"—tinkly laugh—"but somehow you pull it off. I swear I'm not just saying that, either."

Stop. No. Modessa lived inside Milla's brain for long enough. She no longer gets to, and anyway, Milla would far rather think about her *real* friends.

It would have rocked if Milla, Yaz, Katie-Rose, and Violet were in the same class, but since they're not, Milla is glad that each girl has at least one bestie to be with. If Milla was in one class and Yaz, Katie-Rose, and Violet were *all* in the other, Milla doubts she'd survive. She'd wilt, because that's what flowers do when they're sad, and she, Katie-Rose, Violet, and Yasaman *are* flower friends, after all.

Katie-Rose is a flower because of the "rose" part of her name. Violet, obviously, is a violet, and Yasaman means "jasmine" in Turkish. As for herself, a camilla is a small pink flower that grows along the bank of a stream. Gather the four of them in a bouquet, and what do you get? Flower friends forever! *FFFs* instead of *BFFs*, Katie-Rose says.

Milla feels better now. She really does, despite the sad truth that Violet has not yet arrived. No one else in Mr. Emerson's class has gotten here yet, not even Mr. Emerson, who almost always arrives early because he has no life.

That's how *he* puts it, by the way. Not Milla, who adores her goofy teacher and wishes he wouldn't say things like that. But he does, usually following up with a pretend-pitiful monologue about the woes of being a bachelor, with no one to go home to except a dust bunny named Maude. He claims that Maude eats dinner in front of the TV with him (he prefers the History Channel; Maude, supposedly, only likes Nick at Nite), but Milla knows he's being silly.

"Dust bunnies don't eat dinner," someone will invariably point out. Sometimes it's Cole, sometimes it's Thomas. "Dust bunnies don't eat, period."

"Tell that to Maude," Mr. Emerson will respond, shaking his head. "Half my paycheck goes to keeping my pantry stocked with Double Stuf Oreos."

"Which *you* eat," Cole will say. "Admit it, Mr. E. And aren't grown-ups too old to have imaginary friends?"

"Anyway, you have us," one of the girls might say. "Don't we count?"

"Yeah," someone else will toss out. "How can you say you have no life when you have us? That's just heartless."

"Whoa, hold on now," Mr. Emerson will say, holding up his right hand. It's always his right hand that he holds up, because he lost his left hand in a car accident years ago. He lost his entire left arm, all the way up to his shoulder, which is awful. But Milla has never known him any other way.

"I have no life *apart* from being a teacher," he'll clarify. "I get great satisfaction out of being a teacher, and *of course* you count. Listen, I love you guys almost as much as if you were my own students."

"We *are* your students," everybody will chorus, giggling.

"Perhaps," he'll say. "But you aren't waiting for me when I go home, now, are you?"

"Do you *want* us to go to your house?" someone will invariably say.

"Absolutely not," Mr. Emerson will say, wrapping things up. "Which brings us full circle. You kids, as adorable and smelly as you are, can't possibly understand my troubles. Baked goods do occasionally bring me solace, however."

Baked goods, ha. It's such a formal and funny way of putting it.

"Homemade, please, and no craisins," he'll finish. "And absolutely *no* coconut. It's the texture that gets me, not the flavor. Know what I mean?"

Milla tidies her desk as other students trickle in. She keeps an eye out for Violet, but there's someone else she's also antsy to see. A *boy* someone who happens to be adorable and dorky, and whose name is Max, and who wears T-shirts that say things like OBEY GRAVITY! IT'S THE LAW! or 2 + 2 = 5 (FOR EXTREMELY LARGE VALUES OF 2).

Milla has no clue what "extremely large values of

2" means. All she knows is that it's nerdy, and that Max *embraces* that nerdiness. Max is proud of being a nerd, and Milla is proud of Max for being proud of who he is.

Milla is still working on that: on being plain old Milla and feeling good about it. The hardest part is forgiving herself for who she used to be, when she was Modessa's slave. Because when she was Modessa's slave, Milla did bad things. She did them to *Elena*, even.

Last year Modessa said they should all hold their noses whenever Elena walked by, and Milla went along with it. She held her nose and pretended Elena smelled bad, just because Elena has hippy-ish parents who raise llamas on a small farm outside of town. When Modessa said they should call Elena "Llama Girl," Milla went along with that, too. It was so dumb, and anyway, Elena doesn't smell. She didn't then, and she doesn't now.

Why, given all that meanness, was Elena walking arm in arm with Modessa this morning? It makes no sense.

Milla only recently escaped Modessa's head games herself, that's the thing. And what pushed Milla to the breaking point—what made her realize she *had* to get out—was when Modessa turned her cruel gaze on Katie-Rose. Modessa dubbed Katie-Rose a "foster friend" and a waste of space, and she banned Milla from talking to her.

Milla didn't think that was right. No, she *knew* it wasn't right, because why should Modessa get to tell Milla who she could and couldn't talk to? So Milla talked to Katie-Rose anyway . . . when Modessa wasn't around.

But Modessa found out.

To punish Milla, she stole Milla's good luck charm, a small wooden bobblehead turtle named Tally. Then she planted Tally the Turtle in Katie-Rose's backpack, making Milla think that *Katie-Rose* stole Tally. Making *everyone* think Katie-Rose stole Tally.

It was so awful . . . so *so* awful . . . but in a mixed-up, confusing way, Milla is glad it happened, because it was the Fake Incident of the Stolen Turtle (later trimmed to FIST) that brought the flower friends together.

With the help of her new friends, Milla finally found the strength to break Modessa's evil spell. At last she became her own self again.

Milla shivers. The scariest thing about that time in her life—and why she can't help but be scared for Elena— was how easily Modessa cast her spell over Milla in the first place. Or maybe how easily Milla allowed herself to be bewitched? It was as if Milla were a bug trapped in poisoned honey, and the honey tasted sweet, but in a sickly sweet way that was WRONG.

Milla doesn't want Elena to fall into Modessa's trap. At the same time, Milla wants to stay far, far away from Modessa for the sake of self-preservation.

A boy saunters into Mr. Emerson's classroom, pulling her out of her trance. Her heart beats faster. Is it Max? No, it's just Cole, with his long, always-in-his-eyes bangs he's so proud of. Cole used to be nice, Milla thinks, but recently he's been acting stuck-up. Like a *cool kid*, that's the term the FFFs use. Like he thinks he's made of awesome and everyone else is made of stupid. Everyone but the other *cool kids*, that is.

Someone else steps through the door. It's not Max, and it's not Violet, but nonetheless Milla hops to her feet.

"Yaz!" she exclaims. She smiles, because it really is Yaz

here in front of her. Not that there's a fake Yaz running about, or even a Yaz look-alike, but after her run-in, the presence of the real Yaz, solid and familiar, is reassuring.

"Is Violet here?" Yasaman asks.

"Not yet," Milla says.

Yasaman's face falls. Even in the thick of disappointment, she's flat-out gorgeous. Her dark eyes have tiny candles in them—it's her pure soul shining out, Milla thinks—and her hair is glossy and thick. One disobedient strand is visible, but the rest is tucked tidily beneath her *hijab*, which is green and sparkly and sets off Yasaman's warm brown skin.

"But look," Milla says, pulling Yasaman to her desk. "I think Violet's mom will like it, don't you?"

"Wow," Yaz says, admiring the plant on Milla's desk. "What is it called again?"

"A butterfly bush," Milla says. "When Mom Joyce and Mom Abigail bought our house—I wasn't born yet—one of their friends gave *them* a butterfly bush. That's what gave Mom Abigail the idea. That, and the fact that they're so . . . magical, kind of. Like, Mom Joyce didn't believe their butterfly bush would really attract butterflies, even though it had a tag right on it that said, 'Attracts butterflies.' But guess what?"

"What?"

"Two seconds after they planted it—literally, *two seconds*—a butterfly flew into the yard and landed on it." Milla laughs. "Mom Joyce was like, 'You've *got* to be kidding me,' but there it was, the most gorgeous orange-and-black butterfly my moms had ever seen."

"An *awesome* gift," Yasaman says. She touches one of the plant's leaves. "She can look outside and see butterflies whenever she wants, and who can be sad with butterflies around?"

For a moment, the two girls are silent. Yaz catches her bottom lip between her teeth and looks at Milla from under her crazy-long eyelashes, probably worrying if that was a bad thing to say. Sadness, and too much of it, was the reason Violet's mom had to be in the hospital in the first place. It was called being *depressed*, according to Milla's moms. They told Milla that she might not understand, since she was only ten, but that what Violet's mom has (had? since she's home now?) is a *mental* illness and not a *physical* illness.

Thinking about it makes Milla uneasy, because she *does* understand. Milla knows what it's like to feel depressed. When she was part of Modessa's circle, she felt depressed a lot.

Yaz moves her finger from the leaves of the bush to one of its purple blossoms. She's clearly enchanted by the butterfly bush, and Yasaman's shy smile makes Milla feel better. It's so much lovelier to spread happiness than poisoned honey. *That's* what she needs to focus on. That, and making sure Violet is doing all right, given all the changes she has to deal with.

She looks at the door. "Where *is* that girl?"

Mr. Emerson strides into the classroom, whistling. He breaks off when he sees Milla, Yaz, and the enormous potted plant. Gesturing at the plant, he says, "Whoa. Is this a new student?"

Milla giggles, and it loosens things up inside her. "*No.* It's a plant."

Mr. Emerson addresses the butterfly bush. "You're

properly registered, I assume? You've filled out all the paperwork, had your transcripts sent over, etc.?"

Milla and Yaz share a look. Mr. Emerson is tragically embarrassing, but in a cute way. Even his *Woe is me, I'm a lonely bachelor* act is endearing because he's so cheerful about it, despite pretending otherwise. Also, Milla is sure he *does* have a life, and that it's filled to the brim with tons of friends and zero dust bunnies named Maude.

Maybe he doesn't have a girlfriend at the moment, but he'll find someone eventually and fall in love. Milla is sure of it, because he's so great.

"Not the friendliest sort, is he?" Mr. Emerson says to the plant. He squints. "*If* he's a he. Are you a he, new student?"

"It's not a new student," Milla repeats. "It's a *plant*, and you know it."

"*Ahhh*. Perhaps that's why he wants me to *leaf* him alone. *Leaf him alone.* D'ya catch that, girls?"

Milla groans. Yaz scrunches her face as if she'd like to, only she can't—or won't—because she wasn't brought up that way. Her parents are way stricter than Milla's.

Mr. Emerson pats the butterfly bush the way he'd pat a child's head. "Don't worry, buddy, we'll get to the *root* of this."

"Omigosh," Milla says. "Mr. Emerson!"

"And if we have to, we'll get you transplanted to an environment that better suits your needs." He pauses. "Wait—did I say trans*planted*? I meant trans*ferred*. My bad. Though Rivendell *is* quite a fertile learning ground, wouldn't you say, girls?"

"I better go," Yasaman says. She sneaks a peek at Mr. Emerson, who grins. Yaz blushes and hurries across the room. Over her shoulder, she calls, "Say 'hi' to Violet for me, 'kay?"

"Of course," Milla promises.

Only she never gets the chance. Carmen Glover waltzes into the room at eight-thirty on the dot, and Max—*Oh, cute Max!*—follows on her heels.

His shirt today says Factorial! Milla has no idea what that means, but that's okay. Seeing him in his goofy shirt, and not understanding his goofy shirt, is a normal occurrence, and it makes *her* feel normal, just as chatting with Yaz did. She's coming back into herself more and more, and Modessa's sticky residue is clinging to her less and less. Max gives her a shy wave, and she waves back.

Mr. Emerson rings the cowbell he keeps on his desk and tells everyone to take their seats.

"All right, short people with large heads, let's see what the day holds for us," he says. He shakes out a sheet of paper and starts reading the announcements, marking the official start of the school day as well as the official absence of Violet.

Milla cranes her neck toward the hall, but doesn't spot her. She's officially late, all right.

"…and this Friday evening, as you know, all Rivendell students are invited to attend a special event," Mr. Emerson says, and Milla snaps to attention.

The Lock-In, she thinks, knowing already what he's referring to. A surge of energy tingles through her, because all the flower friends are going, and so is Max.

Nighttime! Pajamas! Popcorn! She can hardly hold still.

"If by 'special' you mean 'stupid,'" Cole says under his breath.

Some kids laugh. Ever since the sign-up sheets were passed out last week, the "cool" kids have made it clear that they think the Lock-In is babyish. Someone even passed around a sheet of paper titled "The Top Ten Dorkiest Kids at Rivendell (otherwise known as the top ten reasons NOT to go to the Lock-In)." Milla suspects that a group of cool kids decided together whose names to put down, and in what order, but whoever actually wrote it used block letters to disguise his or her identify. When Mr. Emerson found it, *everyone* claimed innocence.

Katie-Rose topped the list, and to be publicly called out as the number one dorkiest kid at Rivendell *had* to have hurt Katie-Rose's feelings, even though she denied it up and down, backward and forward, sideways and inside-out. That's Katie-Rose's way. She copes with meanness by pretending to be above it. Yet on the day the list circulated, Milla noticed a telltale redness around Katie-Rose's eyes. Milla pretended not to notice, since Katie-Rose clearly didn't want anyone to.

Yasaman made the list, too. Her name filled the seventh-most-dorkiest slot. Milla and Violet weren't on the list, and maybe Milla should have been glad. Instead, it made her feel worse.

But, as Katie-Rose said, the list was idiotic. The only good thing about it was that it meant Modessa and Quin wouldn't be coming to the "babyish" Lock-In, as they surely played a role in composing the list and spreading it around. So too bad for them and all the better for Milla and Katie-Rose and everyone else planning to attend.

Mr. Emerson ignores Cole. "The special event of which I speak is, of course . . ." He twirls his hand, and the non-cool kids fill in the blank.

"The Lock-In!" they call out.

"Bingo! And why is the Lock-In not to be missed?" He whishes his hand through the air and points at Cyril Remkiwicz, who is sullen and not the best kid to choose for audience participation. Mr. Emerson never lets that stop him, however. "Cyril?"

Cyril glares from under a swash of dirty hair. He rarely answers Mr. Emerson's questions. Then again, he rarely answers anyone's questions. He rarely talks, period. When he does, it's only to the handful of humans he tolerates, and of that handful, Violet is at the top of the list, which is strange, freaky, and yet somewhat awesome.

Violet, Violet, Violet. Where are *you?* Milla thinks.

"Right, then," Mr. Emerson says. He swivels his pointing hand, and this time it lands on Milla. Well, not literally. That would be horrifying if his hand flew off his arm and landed—*splat!*—on Milla. "Milla?"

"Huh?" Milla says.

A couple of kids snicker, including Thomas, who is Max's best friend. Max whacks him.

"The Lock-In," Mr. Emerson says. "Tell us, if you would, *why* will it be an evening of such merriment and fun."

"Oh. Um, because you're the one doing it?"

Mr. Emerson's face brightens. "Exactamundo! That's an A plus for you, Camilla, and a free homework pass to go along with it."

"Aw!" Cole complains. "Not fair!"

"With me at the helm, I guarantee the Lock-In will be a blast," Mr. Emerson says. His eyebrows come together.

"Oh. And the lovely Mrs. Gundeck will be chaperoning as well."

Groans rise. Mrs. Gundeck is not lovely. Mrs. Gundeck teaches German, and she threatens to spank her students' *Hinterns*—or bottoms—when they fidget or can't stop clicking their pens.

"Ah, Mrs. Gundeck has a fun side," Mr. Emerson says cheerfully. "She must."

Must she? Milla wonders. It's far more likely, she suspects, that Mrs. Gundeck has a doesn't-actually-like-children side, as well as a children-are-germy-and-gross side. More than once, Mrs. Gundeck has sent a student to the bathroom to wash up, accusing him or her of smelling sweaty or having Dorito-breath. She frequently complains of being unusually sensitive to anything "distasteful," from strong odors to smushed spiders to toe jam. She's so sensitive, in fact, that the mere mention of toe jam makes her feel faint.

Milla knows this to be true, as she has seen with her own two eyes Mrs. Gundeck nearly faint. While Rivendell's fifth graders are split into two classes—either Mr.

Emerson's class or Ms. Perez's—the kids from each class get mixed up and switched around when it comes to "specials," like PE and art and German. Milla figures it's so everyone gets to know one another.

Anyway, Milla and Katie-Rose aren't in the same primary class, but they do have German together. Last Thursday, Mrs. Gundeck was teaching a lesson about German folk tales when Katie-Rose, out of the blue, exclaimed, "Omigosh, there is actual *mold* between my toes!"

Her announcement caused a kerfuffle, of course.

"Omigod, *so* vile," Modessa said.

"No way," Chance said, slapping his knee. "Show us! Is it green?"

Mrs. Gundeck, at the front of the room, turned as pasty as a piece of Wonderbread. Her eyes bulged, her chest heaved, and she put her hand over her mouth. *She almost vomited.* Katie-Rose's hypothetical toe jam made Mrs. Gundeck almost vomit.

As for *why* Katie-Rose was examining her toes during class, or why she would find it normal to announce the presence of toe-jam mold to the entire class ... Well, that's an entirely different issue.

"We'll have pizza, watch a movie, play some games," Mr. Emerson says. "And there are a few spaces left, so if you haven't signed up, it's not too late." He grins. "Be there or be square."

"I think you mean be there *and* be square," Cole mutters.

This time, Mr. Emerson chooses not to ignore him. "What's that?" he asks.

Cole blinks. "Nothing."

"Didn't sound like nothing. Come on, out with it."

The atmosphere in the room takes on a charge. Mr. Emerson is a fabulous teacher, possibly the fabulous-est. But he can be fierce behind the glint of his smile. He doesn't put up with meanness or negative attitudes.

Mr. Emerson waits.

Seconds tick by.

Cole sighs loudly. "Okay, and I say this with no disrespect, but who wants to go to *school* on a Friday night? You'd have to be kind of a loser, wouldn't you?"

"I'll be here Friday night," Mr. Emerson says. "Am I a loser?"

Cole's face turns red. Even though Mr. Emerson pokes fun at himself—saying he has no life, making up dust bunny companions named Maude—no one else makes fun of him. Not even the cool kids.

"You have to be there," Cole says. "It's your job."

"I volunteered, actually." Mr. Emerson sweeps his gaze over the rest of the class. "It's going to be a good time. Come."

He strolls to the whiteboard. "And now for something almost as thrilling, let's pull out our *Wordly Wise* books, shall we?"

Milla raises her hand.

"Yes, Milla?"

"Um . . . do you know why Violet isn't here? Is she sick?" Milla asks. When kids miss a day of school, their parents are supposed to call the office and tell Mr. McGreevy. Then Mr. McGreevy passes along the news to the teachers.

Mr. Emerson furrows his brow, and Milla gets the sense that he hasn't noticed Violet's absence until now.

"Maybe she's got the stomach flu," Carmen Glover says. "My aunt says it's going around."

"I'll check with Mr. McGreevy during morning break," Mr. Emerson tells Milla. "But I'm sure she's fine." He uncaps an erasable marker. "Turn to lesson sixteen, please. Carmen, would you do us the honor of reading paragraph one?"

Carmen reads aloud in her nasal voice. The passage is about a homeless shelter and the people who live there, but Milla can't focus. Plus, there's a ginormous butterfly bush on her desk, leaving little room for her *Wordly Wise* book.

She wraps her arm around the pot, heaves it up, and places it beside her on the floor. She has more space now. Still, she feels crowded. Or, no. Squished. Like her heart doesn't have enough room in her rib cage. Like it's trapped.

She tells herself she's worried about Violet, and that it's normal to be worried, because Violet is dealing with some hard stuff. It would be abnormal *not* to be worried.

Yet try as she might to pretend otherwise, Milla knows there's more bothering her than that. Yes, Milla is worried about Violet. But Violet isn't the only person

Milla's worried about, and the "trapped" feeling she's experiencing?

Well . . . it isn't new. It's how she felt when she was with Modessa. *Exactly.*

She pushes her fingers to her temples, troubled by the memory of Elena's wide, blinking eyes. Troubled by the notion that sometimes you can choose what to run away from, but other times, maybe, you can't. And just say a girl *is* trapped—or not even a girl, necessarily. Pretend, for the sake of argument, that *any*one is trapped: man, boy, girl, or child. If a fellow human being is trapped, and you know it, is it an option to look away?

It's a question Milla wishes she could un-ask.

✿ Two ✿

Yasaman

Yasaman adores her fifth-grade teacher, Ms. Perez. She's nice and funny, and she's always willing to listen when Yaz has a problem. She gives good advice, too. Plus, Ms. Perez is *soooo* pretty. She's got glossy brown hair and sparkling eyes and a teasing smile, and she wears stylish clothes—usually skirts and cute tops— which she pairs with unfailingly stylish shoes, the sort of shoes that Yasaman admires and yet suspects she'll never be able to wear, because she'd trip.

It's true that Ms. Perez is on the chubby side, but

Yasaman doesn't care about that. Yasaman doesn't think *any*one should care, especially not Ms. Perez herself. Ms. Perez does, though. She's not happy with the way she looks, and the way Yasaman can tell is because whenever Yaz compliments her, Ms. Perez finds a way to not fully accept it. This morning Yaz told Ms. Perez how much she liked her gold hoop earrings, and Ms. Perez sort of laughed and said, "Well, with earrings, it's hard to go *too* terribly wrong." Then she caught herself—that's how Yasaman read it—and added, "But thank you, Yasaman. What a sweet thing to say."

"I'm not just saying it," Yaz insisted. "They're beautiful." She wanted to say more: that Ms. Perez herself is beautiful, and she shouldn't be so hard on herself, and that one day she *will* find her "Mr. Right," despite her glum prediction that she won't.

Yasaman knows this very private detail about Ms. Perez because she heard Ms. Perez talking about it to Ms. Viney, the art teacher. Yaz wasn't eavesdropping. She just happened to come in from morning recess to get a drink of water one day, and since the water fountain is next to the art room, and Ms. Perez happened to be *in* the art room, chatting with Ms. Viney, well, Yaz couldn't help but overhear.

It was girl talk between two friends, not teacher talk between teachers. It wasn't meant for students' ears.

But it went into Yasaman's ears anyway, and it reminded her of an idea Yaz had had a while ago, but never did anything about. Maybe now's the time?

Ms. Perez has always been extraspecial nice to Yaz, after all. Yaz would never say this out loud, but she's pretty sure she's Ms. Perez's favorite student. Never before this year has Yaz been any teacher's favorite. Usually she's "smart, quiet, well-behaved Yasaman" and nothing more.

She wants to be something more. She longs and yearns and aches to be something more . . . only she's not sure what that "something more" would be, exactly. Or how to make it happen. How to *become* more, in the way that some things—caterpillars transforming into butterflies, for example—do so easily.

Certain things *are* easy for Yasaman. Computers,

math, knowing right from wrong. But other things are hard, like wanting to stretch and grow, but not knowing how. Yaz wonders if the "not knowing how" part is related to another aspect of her identity—namely, the "being different from everyone else" part.

Ms. Perez is different from everyone else, too, and maybe this is why she and Yasaman have such a strong connection. Yasaman is different because of her religion. She and her little sister, Nigar, are the only Muslim kids at Rivendell. Ms. Perez is different because of her appearance. Thousand Oaks, California, is bursting at the seams with slender blond women who do yoga every day, while Ms. Perez is just plain bursting at the seams. That's Ms. Perez's joke, not Yasaman's.

But no, Ms. Perez is not blond and skinny. She's a brown-haired Hispanic woman who has curves and round rosy cheeks and an overall . . . *softness*. Soft is good, Yasaman thinks.

In the fashion magazines her cousin Hulya buys and hides in her sock drawer, the models are so brittle and hard-edged that Yaz feels bad for them. Sometimes they look mean with their jutting elbows and cocked hips and too-sharp cheekbones, and sometimes they look hungry. Sometimes both. If someone were to hug them, they look like they might snap right in half.

Not Ms. Perez. Ms. Perez is the perfect softness for hugs, and that brings Yaz back to her excellent but so far un-acted-upon idea:

Ms. Perez's "Mr. Right" could be Mr. Emerson. It's perfect. It's glorious! They're both single, they're both super cool (in a good way, not a too-cool-for-school way), *and they both live right here at Rivendell, practically.* Not really, but close enough.

If they got married, they could carpool together!

If they had kids, their kids could attend Rivendell and be with their mom and dad every day! And if they ever needed time away from Rivendell and their kids, Yasaman could babysit for them!!!!

Yaz shivers with the deliciousness of it. She needs to come up with specific matchmaking strategies. She'll get Violet, Milla, and Katie-Rose to put on their thinking caps, too. Plan Teacherly Lurve ... activate!

In the meantime, Yaz will bask in the pleasure of being Ms. Perez's favorite student, a position that comes with secret perks. Like right now, she's organizing Ms. Perez's bookshelf, since she finished her math quiz early and turned it in before the rest of the class. Some kids might not see organizing a bookshelf as a perk, but that's why they're not Ms. Perez's favorites.

Yasaman studies the jumble of books jammed willy-nilly onto the shelves. She taps her lip with the knuckle of her thumb. Ms. Perez's desk is only three or four feet away, so she leans over and whispers, "Alphabetical or by subject matter? Or by reading level—that's another way you could go. What do you think?"

Ms. Perez glances up from last week's vocabulary tests, which she's grading. "Um . . . alphabetical," she says. She returns to her stack of papers, but having been interrupted, she seems to have lost her flow. She puts down her pen, which is purple. Ms. Perez always grades in purple, never red.

"Hey," she whispers. "Do you think we could sneak out and go to Starbucks instead?"

Yaz smiles.

"I'm serious," Ms. Perez says. "I *hate* grading. I hate it with a mad passion that makes me want to throw dishes at someone. Or vocabulary books."

"I'll grade them for you if you want," Yaz offers.

"I might take you up on that," Ms. Perez says.

Yaz glows. She *is* an excellent grader. She rocks at spelling, and she has neat, teacherly handwriting.

Katie-Rose, on the other hand, has deplorable hand-writing. When Katie-Rose turns in an assignment, it looks as if it's been attacked by a pencil-wielding raccoon. Katie-Rose doesn't care about neat handwriting. She only cares about getting the answers right, which she does.

Modessa struts to the front of the room to turn her quiz in. She gives Yasaman a disdainful glance as she passes. Yasaman doesn't drop her eyes as she once would have, but it takes effort. Modessa is mean, and one of the people she enjoys being mean to is Yasaman.

The same is true of Modessa's best friend, Quin. And speak of devil—or *iti an çomaği hazirla!*, as her *baba* would say—here comes Quin to turn her quiz in.

"Brownnoser," Quin whispers to Yasaman.

Yasaman is too classy to respond, but . . . *yuck*. They leave a bad taste in her mouth. Plus they're supposed to read quietly or work on homework until everyone is done, but they don't. They put their heads together and whisper, bothering the kids who are still working.

Ms. Perez glances in their direction, and they shush. But the second Ms. Perez returns to her grading, Modessa and Quin return to their whispering. Modessa fishes something out of her backpack. A book. She doesn't read it, but passes it to Quin. They whisper *and* snicker, and then—*uh-oh*—they swivel their heads toward a girl named Elena.

Yasaman's stomach clenches. They better leave Elena alone, or she'll . . . she'll . . . well, she doesn't know what she'll do. But Elena is a sweet girl, and she played a crucial role in the Snack Attack the flower friends launched last month. Elena was a hero, really, and Yaz will always be grateful.

The target of the Snack Attack was the snack passed out to Rivendell's students during morning break. Every day it was the same: a handful of bright orange crackers called Cheezy D'Lites, which had zero grams of cheese per serving but were chock-full of partially hydrogenated cottonseed oil and orange dye. The goal of the Snack Attack was to get rid of those Cheezy D'Lites, thus making Rivendell a Cheezy D'Lites–free zone.

Without exactly mentioning their true agenda, the flower friends got permission from the principal to give a schoolwide presentation about staying healthy. Then Katie-Rose gave a stirring speech about the evils of factory farms, and Elena, whom Milla had asked to bring her potbelly pig, Porkchop, to the assembly, stepped forward to show the school what a healthy pig looked like.

Porkchop was a big hit. A two-hundred pound hit, to be exact, but in the end things got slightly chaotic, because two annoying boys named Preston and Chance added an unsanctioned dead-chicken dance to the presentation, and Porkchop got upset and escaped from Elena's grasp and galloped all over Rivendell's commons, snorting and grunting and making the preschoolers shriek.

Regardless, Porkchop was a champ, and Elena was a

champ for bringing him. So yay, Elena! And *boo*, Modessa and Quin. *Boo* for whisper-snickering in Elena's direction when they've already made fun of her plenty.

They *keep* whisper-snickering, and then—*uh-oh*. Modessa does an eyeball thrust at Quin, a bossy eyeball thrust that seems to mean *go on, stupid*, and Quin reaches over and taps Elena's shoulder. Elena jumps, and Yasaman presses her lips together.

Quin gives Elena the book from Modessa's backpack. Elena looks at it, and spots of color rise on her cheeks. She tries to return the book to Quin, but Quin sits on her hands. Elena leans out of her seat and tries to make Modessa take the book, but Modessa looks hard at Elena and shakes her head.

Just put it on her desk! Yasaman urges Elena silently. *Who cares if Modessa officially accepts it? If it's meant to humiliate you or get you in trouble, which I'm sure it is, then just get rid of it, whatever it is!*

Modessa scribbles something on a scrap of paper, balls it up, and tosses it onto Elena's desk. Elena uncrumples the note and skims it. Elena is a farm girl, which means she spends a lot of time outside, which means her skin is tanned even in October. Yasaman has never seen Elena look pale, and she wouldn't have thought it possible if she didn't see it with her own eyes. But Elena's face, flushed and ruddy just moments ago, drains of color.

Modessa's lips curve up. Her expression reminds Yaz of Hulya's hungry fashion models.

Yasaman fidgets. Should she go to Ms. Perez and tell her that something's going on, something not good? But what would she say? She doesn't know what they're up to. She has no proof that they're up to *any*thing.

They are, though. Modessa jabs Quin, who jabs Elena. Elena slides out of her seat, her shoulders hunched so high that they practically graze her ears. She grips the book. Her knuckles are white. Her fingertips, to make up for it, are purply-red.

Elena, no! Yaz thinks. Her muscles poise as if she might spring to her feet, which is alarming, because Yasaman's not a spring-to-her-feet sort of girl. She's a watch-and-listen girl, and right this second, she's also a heart-in-her-throat girl. She wants to stop whatever bad thing Modessa is setting Elena up for from happening, but she doesn't know how. A job like this is much more suited for Katie-Rose, only Katie-Rose is bent over her math quiz, scrawling her raccoon scribbles.

Elena walks to the front of the room. She walks to Ms. Perez's desk, and Yasaman experiences a *whoosh* of relief. She should have trusted Elena to be able to take care of herself. She should have trusted Elena to be brave enough to tell on Modessa and Quin, even if they *are* Modessa and Quin.

Elena hesitates, then drops the book onto Ms. Perez's desk. Yasaman is light-headed and almost wants to laugh.

"It's for you," Elena tells Ms. Perez in a faint voice.

Huh? Yasaman frowns, because that's not what you say when you turn in a contraband book. That's what you say when you give someone a gift. *Is Elena . . . ? Why would Elena . . . ?*

From the back row, Modessa clears her throat. Elena glances over her shoulder, and Modessa does an eyeball thrust that leaves no room for misunderstanding. *Do it,* Modessa's eyeball thrust means.

Yasaman's heart flops as she realizes that whatever

cruelty Modessa has in mind involves not only Elena, but her beloved teacher as well.

"It's, um, a present," Elena says. She sweeps her arm out. "From all of us. From the whole class."

No, it's not! Whatever that book is, it's not from the whole class, and it's definitely not from Yaz. She tries to speak. Not even a squeak comes out.

"Really?" Ms. Perez says, and because it's Elena who's giving it to her, she doesn't suspect a trap. She picks up the book, and Yaz knows what will happen next. Ms. Perez will read the title out loud, because that's what regular people do when they're given a gift and have no reason to suspect foul play.

"The Black Book of Hollywood Diet Secrets," Ms. Perez reads aloud. She inhales sharply, and Modessa and Quin titter. Elena twines her hands around each other, around and around and around.

Yasaman feels helpless. She doesn't know how to save her teacher.

"How lovely," Ms. Perez says, and Yaz furrows her brow. Elena stops her twining.

Ms. Perez has the attention of the whole class by now,

which is surely part of Modessa's plan. But Ms. Perez smiles. She smiles! She holds the book face-out so that everyone can see, then turns it back and flips to a random page. She reads a paragraph or two to herself, or pretends to. She turns the page. Her eyebrows go up.

"Oh my," she says. Her eyebrows form full-on peaks. "Oh *my*."

Modessa's legs are crossed, and she pumps her top foot up and down. Her prank isn't playing out as she hoped, it seems. As for Yasaman, her chest is tight, but not as tight as it was. She's not sure what Ms. Perez is up to, but she seems to be quite capable of saving herself.

She flips another page, and her eyes widen. "Well, what do you know," she murmurs. "I *never* would have guessed that."

Modessa can't stand it. "You never would have guessed *what?*" she demands.

Ms. Perez lifts her head. "Hmm? I'm afraid I got distracted."

Modessa huffs. "What does it *say?* The book we gave you?"

Ms. Perez crinkles her nose at Modessa, as if Modessa

is just the cutest thing ever. "Oh, nothing you don't already know, a skinny thing like you."

Modessa blinks. Elena, meanwhile, slinks away from Ms. Perez's desk, scooting sideways along the wall and ending up by the reading nook. Her foot bumps Yaz's beanbag, and she almost stumbles. She glances down, and her eyes widen when she sees Yasaman's expression.

Neither "quiet" nor "well-behaved" comes close to describing how Yasaman feels. "Furious" is closer, but even "furious" isn't enough.

"*Why?*" Yaz mouths, hoping Elena can sense the full heat of her disdain.

Flustered, Elena hurries to her seat, while at the front of the room, Ms. Perez keeps reading the book, or pretending to.

"So many tips in here," she murmurs. "And you think I need *all* this help, Elena and Modessa?"

Elena's eyes fly to Modessa. Modessa folds her arms over her chest. Quin doesn't seem to know how to react. Should she feel lucky Ms. Perez didn't call out her name, or jealous that she called out Elena's?

"Uh, whatever," Brannen says, tilting back on the rear

legs of his chair. "But just so you know, I don't get why Elena said that book's from all of us. It's not from me, and I don't know why you need help, anyway."

"Yeah" and "It's not from me, either," say most of the kids in the class. They chirp their innocence like baby birds, and Yasaman chirps along with them. So does Katie-Rose. Everyone wants Ms. Perez to know that they had nothing to do with *The Black Book of Hollywood Diet Secrets.*

"Wait," Ms. Perez says. "So is it just from Elena and Modessa, then?" She scans the room. "If anyone else chipped in, speak up. I certainly want to give credit where credit's due."

Quin sinks in her seat.

Modessa opens her mouth, perhaps thinking to claim that she, too, knew nothing about the book until this second. Then she scowls. She's probably remembering that she gave up any claim to innocence when she asked, "What does it say, the book *we* gave you?"

She mirrors Quin's slumped posture.

"I see," Ms. Perez says. "Well, thank you, Modessa and Elena. I'll write you an actual thank-you note, of course, as

I'm a big believer in good manners. Or, no, I'll write your *parents* a letter, because parents always enjoy hearing nice things about their children, don't they?"

She smiles. It is a teacherly smile that says, *Perhaps you're not as clever as you think you are, are you?*

Modessa looks livid, as if Ms. Perez set out to shame her instead of the other way around. Elena's bottom lip trembles as if she might cry.

"All right, class," Ms. Perez says, closing the awful book about dieting. "You've got five minutes to finish your tests, so get back to work, please."

Throughout the room, kids do as she suggested, with two noteworthy exceptions. Well, three, counting Yasaman. But Yasaman's not interested in her own reaction. She's interested in the reactions of Katie-Rose, who rotates one-hundred-and-eighty degrees in her seat to gaze at Modessa, and Modessa, who seems unable to resist the laser beam intensity of Katie-Rose's gloat.

Katie-Rose and Modessa have a "history," just as Yasaman and Modessa do. What Yasaman endured was relentlessly humiliating, but what Katie-Rose suffered through was worse.

Yasaman watches Katie-Rose smile at Modessa, and—*HA!*—Katie-Rose so totally wins their face-off, because *omigosh*, Modessa loses her composure and sticks out her tongue.

Katie-Rose plops back into her seat. She gives Yasaman a gleeful thumbs-up.

When morning break rolls around, Yasaman lingers in the classroom as the other kids rush out to the playground. She approaches Ms. Perez's desk. She holds on to it and tucks her foot behind the opposite calf.

Are you okay? she wants to ask. *You put up a good front—a really good front—but . . . are you okay?*

Ms. Perez gestures for Yaz to come around her desk. She scoots over on her chair, pats the smooth wood, and says, "Here, sit with me for a minute."

Yaz perches on the far side of the seat. She doesn't want to crowd Ms. Perez. Ms. Perez puts her arm around Yaz and gives her a squeeze.

"Are you all right, sweetie?" she says.

"*Me?*" Yaz says. "*I'm* fine." Her gaze drifts to the *The Black Book of Hollywood Diet Secrets.* "But that *book . . .*"

"Grade-A trash," Ms. Perez proclaims. She sweeps

the book into the garbage can, and it makes a satisfying clunk.

"Still, I am so *so* sorry," Yaz says.

"You played no role in that ridiculous prank," Ms. Perez says. "I *was* surprised Elena was involved, though."

"Me, too."

"Oh, well," Ms. Perez says. She sighs. "Hopefully those girls will grow up one day, but until then? They're kids. I can take 'em."

"Yeah," Yaz says. It comes out tiny, and she clears her throat. "You go, girlfriend."

Ms. Perez laughs.

"Seriously. You're like . . . a superhero."

"If only. Maybe I *should* read that silly book."

"No!" Yaz cries. "You're beautiful, Ms. Perez. Beautiful *and* brave!"

Ms. Perez gazes out the window. She's silent for such a long time that Yasaman wants to hit something, she's so frustrated. Not that she would, because along with so many other *nots*, Yasaman is not a hitting sort of girl.

She *is* the sort of girl who can't stand to see her teacher sad, and she doubles—*quadruples*—her determination to fix that problem. She will do whatever it takes to make other people see how wonderful Ms. Perez is. People like Mr. Emerson, who is surely Ms. Perez's Mr. Right, even if he doesn't yet know it.

"Um . . . Ms. Perez?" she says after the no-talking has gone on so long she can't stand it anymore.

Ms. Perez turns back to Yasaman. Her eyes are shiny. "Thank you, sweet Yaz."

❊ Three ❊

Katie-Rose

A t lunch, Katie-Rose pulls bits of crust off her peanut butter and jelly sandwich as Yasaman tells Katie-Rose and Milla about *The Black Book of Hollywood Diet Secrets*. They're eating in the commons because the teachers said it was too windy to eat outside, but Katie-Rose would have put up with even the loudest, windiest wind—happily!—if it meant not having to listen to this conversation.

And yet Yasaman can't stop saying how shocked she is that out of all the people in the world, it was *Elena* who gave the mean prank book to Ms. Perez.

Katie-Rose doesn't like what happened in class any more than Yasaman, although she is *glad* that Ms. Perez pulled a fast one and made Modessa and Elena look stupid instead. Aside from that, she has no interest in discussing the incident. It's over and in the past, the end.

But Yasaman props her elbow on the table and her chin on her palm. "I mean, *Elena*?" she marvels again. "It's just ... it's just—"

"Shocking?" Katie-Rose supplies.

"Yeah," she says. "I just don't understand why Elena would do that. I don't understand why anyone would, but especially Elena. You know?"

"Totally," Milla says. "Elena's never been friends with Modessa and Quin."

"No, she's always been *un*-friends with them," Yaz says. "That's why I'm so shocked."

Katie-Rose rolls her eyes, but mainly to herself. Yasaman always sees the best in people, which for the most part is endearing. But sometimes? It's *shockingly* annoying.

Milla doesn't respond, but instead bites neatly into

the cucumber and mint sandwich her Mom Abigail made her. The bread is homemade, and the sandwich is cut into four identical triangles. It's already crust-free. Her mom made it that way.

Yasaman exhales. "Modessa and Quin haven't ever even been nice to Elena, have they? If anything, wouldn't you say they've been deliberately *un*-nice to her?"

Un-friends. *Un*-nice. Shocking, shocking, shocking— except for the small, tiny fact that if Yaz and Milla would open their eyes, they'd see it isn't shocking at all. It's bizarre that Milla, especially, doesn't see it. Unless she really *is* play acting?

No, she can't be. If she is, that means she's, like, deliberately pretending not to remember her history with Modessa, a horrible, hurtful history that happened to involve Katie-Rose in a very *un-nice* way. Oh, and Yaz was there, too. She witnessed it all.

Sure, Yasaman is made of sugar and spice and everything nice, and sure, Yaz always wants to think the best of people. But there will always be people, like Modessa, who are just rotten, and other people, like Elena, who do their rotten bidding. That won't change. Or . . . it *probably* won't change. It probably definitely won't change. Only the idea of "change" is tricky and confusing.

Like, what if—one day—things change for the FFF's? Not that Katie-Rose doesn't trust her friends . . . *but*. Based on a list passed from student to student last week, Katie-Rose is dorky. In fact, based on that same stupid list, Katie-Rose is *the number one most dorky girl in the whole school*, to which Katie-Rose said loudly, "Fine. Dorks rule."

She also cried, though. In the girls' room during morning break, and at home that night under her bed. She and the dust bunnies had a good ol' cry, and then she crawled out and brushed herself off and vowed never to think about that stupid list again.

She didn't quite succeed at that vow, and it comes back to haunt her more often than seems fair. It's poking at her brain right now, for example, as Yaz and Milla go *blah-blah-blah* about Elena (who didn't get put on the dork list), and Modessa (who surely played a big role in creating the dork list).

Katie-Rose's deeply buried fear, which is probably crazy, which is probably *definitely* crazy . . .

Well, what if her friends realize that the list is right, and that Modessa is right, and that Katie-Rose is a dork who will never know the cool thing to do or wear or say? What if Katie-Rose *can't* change, even if she wants to, but her friends can?

She drags her hand over her face. She knows this will never happen, but just say her FFFs get it into their heads that *they* should change. Awful things rise from the depths of her subconscious: makeup, purses, panty hose. Boys. (And that one? The boys one? It actually has happened—just look at Milla and Max.)

But, again. Just say her FFFs go nuts, arriving at school one of these mornings in fishnet stockings and bright red lipstick. Or say it's a Saturday, and Katie-Rose says, "Hey! Let's go see a movie!" only to have Violet say, "Ooo, I've got a better idea. Let's go BRA SHOPPING!"

If her FFFs decide to change . . . well . . . what if they leave Katie-Rose behind?

"Maybe I'm overreacting," Yasaman says, halfheartedly stabbing at her falafel. "Maybe Elena . . . I don't know. Didn't know what she was doing?"

Fat chance, Katie-Rose thinks, but doesn't say. She

agrees that Yaz is overreacting, however, and it offers her an unexpected ray of hope. If Yaz is overreacting, maybe Katie-Rose is, too. Apparently, she sometimes does that. Frankly, she doesn't see it, but there are a fair amount of life details that she and other people view differently. For example? She honestly doesn't mind long toenails, which everyone else seems to find disgusting. She finds potato chip sandwiches delicious, while the smell of most perfumes makes her want to barf.

She makes herself take a bite of her sandwich, the soft, yummy, inside part, and she tries to view the Modessa/Elena situation from a more *mature* perspective. "Not everything is black and white," her mom is always telling her, to which she likes to reply, "Oh, yeah? What about Oreos? Or zebras? Or zebras eating Oreos?"

"And she likes animals!" Yaz wails. "Remember when she brought in her photo album? And under each llama's picture was the llama's name and favorite type of grass or hay or whatever?"

"I'm sorry, but what does that have to do with anything?" Katie-Rose says.

"Well . . . because she likes *animals*," Yaz repeats. "People who like animals are *nice*."

"Dudes," she says, "not to burst your bubble, but liking animals means nothing, not in this situation. Elena is Medusa's new recruit. Okay?"

"*Recruit?*" Milla says. Her eyes are round and so, so blue.

Katie-Rose's stomach hurts. Eating even that one bite of sandwich was a mistake, and it crosses her mind that there's a negative to being *mature*. Stomachaches. Ulcers. Tums, which her dad takes for his heartburn.

"Could we not talk about Modessa, please?" she says at last. "I'm worried about Violet. Where *is* she?"

Finally, Milla and Yaz stop with their Elena-blathering. Yasaman blushes, and Milla bows her head. Training her gaze on the tidy triangles of her sandwich, she says, "Um . . . I asked Mr. Emerson, but he didn't know if she was sick or not."

"I talked to her yesterday before she and her dad went to pick up her mom," Yaz offers. "She wasn't sick then."

"Maybe she overslept?" Milla suggests.

Natalia Totenburg, a girl Katie-Rose is trying to be

nicer to, appears at their table and drops into a vacant seat, even though lunch is half over and even though none of the flower friends said, "Hey! Natalia! Come on over and sit with us, you delightful specimen of humanity!"

Natalia takes a container of weird green noodles out of her lunch box, along with a pair of chopsticks. Katie-Rose disapproves. Chopsticks? Really?

"Maybe she overslept," Milla repeats. "And then, like, her mom couldn't bring her, since she doesn't know the roads and stuff yet. And her dad had already gone to work."

"We're talking about Violet," Yasaman tells Natalia. "Yesterday Violet's mom came home from"—she hesitates—"the, um, hospital."

"Ohhhh," Natalia says. "*Right.*" Most of the kids in the fifth grade know about Violet's mom being in California Regional's mental ward, just as they know that Becca's parents are divorced and Milla has two moms.

Fifth graders aren't very big on "showing discretion," as Katie-Rose's mom would say. Katie-Rose would put it another way: Fifth graders have big mouths. Natalia, in particular, has a big mouth, although only half of her big mouth has to do with being a gossip girl. The other half is her ginormous headgear, with all of its rubber bands and metal hooks and snappy things, and the *other* other half is just plain Natalia.

And fine, that brings Natalia up to one-and-a-half big mouths. Whatever. It fits. Last month she used her too-big mouth to try and claim ownership of the flower friends' Snack Attack campaign, and she tried to claim ownership of Yasaman as well. She didn't succeed—*der*—but her meddling caused problems between Katie-Rose and Yasaman.

They worked everything out eventually, but Yasaman (again, *always* insisting on seeing the best in everyone) made Katie-Rose promise to give Natalia a chance. According to Yasaman, Natalia is just a lonely girl who wants to have friends and be part of a group, and Katie-Rose shouldn't call her "lint," even though "lint" is the perfect nickname for a girl who clings and clings and refuses to let go.

Katie-Rose imagines a giant clump of lint wearing a giant headgear. She giggles.

Natalia lifts a noodle with her chopsticks. "What if

Violet'th mom had a relapth?" Natalia says, meaning *relapse*. Her headgear makes her lisp.

Katie-Rose stops giggling. "No way," she says. "There's no way Violet's mom had a relapse, because the hospital people wouldn't have let her go if there was even the tiniest chance of that happening."

Milla gnaws her thumbnail. She shares an anxious glance with Yaz.

"*Stop*," Katie-Rose tells them. She shoots Natalia a look to say, *See what you've done?*

Natalia shrugs, and the noodle dangling from her chopsticks sways.

"We'll talk to Violet tonight, and she'll explain why she wasn't here, and it'll be something dumb and totally innocent," Katie-Rose says.

"Like what?" Milla asks.

"Like . . . maybe the hospital beds had bedbugs," she says. "And Violet's mom's clothes got infested, and so they had to boil every article of clothing in the whole house, and also the sheets, and Violet volunteered to stay home and help."

Milla, Yasaman, and Natalia stare at her.

"Or maybe she just wanted some time alone with her mom," Katie-Rose says. Her stomach feels better, enough so that she gives her PB&J another go.

"Well, why didn't she call one of us and say so?" Milla says.

"How should I know?" Katie-Rose replies with her mouth full. She swallows and unsticks her tongue from the top of her mouth with a *slurp*. Natalia may have exotic green noodles with fancy chopsticks, but there is nothing like the satisfying glue-y sound of peanut butter mixed with spit mixed with mouth flesh.

Milla glances at the clock over the mural. "Lunch is over. We better get to class."

"Okey-doke," Katie-Rose says, happy to move on since it hasn't been the funnest lunch. She stuffs the remains of her sandwich into her brown paper bag and crumples the bag into a ball. Oh, and there is an uneaten plum in there, too. Katie-Rose feels the hardness of it within the crumple-ball. *Farewell, plum*, she thinks as she lobs the bag at the trash can by the water fountain.

Unfortunately, she misses, and instead of landing in the trash can, her lunch bag makes contact with the head of an extremely annoying boy named Preston, whose favorite pastime is throwing erasers at Katie-Rose. Or scraps of paper or carrot sticks or anything. One time? He threw a stinky, disgusting, balled-up sock at her! And it was his sock, which he found when Ms. Perez made them clean out their desks one day!

So while Katie-Rose is embarrassed that she missed the trash can, it is delightful payback that she got in such a clean shot at Preston's head.

"Hey!" Preston cries. He feels the back of his head. He looks down and sees the lunch blob. Katie-Rose follows his gaze and sees that the plum seems to have burst. Preston's eyes widen. So do Katie-Rose's.

"Uh-oh," Milla says.

"Oopsy daisy," Katie-Rose says, not meaning it a bit.

Preston turns. He spots Katie-Rose.

"Maybe you should run," Yaz says.

"Never," Katie-Rose says. *This* is what being a kid is about. *This* is the beauty of not being mature.

Preston sets his jaw, wipes his hand on his jeans, and strides her way. Katie-Rose presses her lips together to keep them from twitching or smiling or wobbling in some weird way.

"You threw your lunch at me," he accuses, standing above her and appearing quite tall.

"No, you blocked my shot," Katie-Rose responds.

"You hit me in the head," Preston says.

"You stuck your head in the way of my lunch."

"My hair is all sticky."

"My *lunch* is all hairy. How am I supposed to eat it now?"

His brow furrows. "You threw it away."

"I *tried* to throw it away, sure. But you ruined that, didn't you?"

"Well … well … you owe me a new bottle of shampoo!" Preston says.

Oh, please. As if boys like Preston even wash their hair.

Then her brain pulls a fast one on her, dredging up a long-forgotten memory of taking a seat behind Preston one day and noticing, before she realized it was Preston, that his hair looked clean and shiny and soft enough to pet. *Blegh*. She shoves the memory back into the cage where it belongs.

"I am not buying you new shampoo," she pronounces. She rises from her seat. "If anything, you owe me a new lunch. And before you ask, I prefer strawberry. Jam, not jelly. And now if you'll *excuse* me, some of us have places to be. So good-bye."

Chin held high, she takes off for Ms. Perez's classroom, forgetting in the heat of the moment that Preston is in Ms. Perez's class, too. She remembers ten seconds later, when he saunters in with his plum-juice-spiked hair.

She feigns indifference. She clasps her hands on her desk and pretends to listen as Ms. Perez starts in on some boring something-or-other. It has to do with homework, so it's not like it matters. Katie-Rose knows she can get all As even if she spaces out occasionally.

Katie-Rose tunes in when Ms. Perez utters the word *trapeze*, however. And not just *trapeze*, but *trapeze lessons*. She sits up straight. Did Ms. Perez really just mention trapeze lessons? Here, at Rivendell, involving an actual flesh-and-blood trapeze, which will be set up in the PE room???

Ms. Perez turns toward the door of the classroom. She steps halfway out and says, "Oh good, you found us." She ushers in a slim girl with freckles and red hair. The girl is older than fifth grade. She's probably in high school, even. She's holding a sheaf of papers.

"Come on in, Josie," Ms. Perez says. "Class, this is Josie Sanders. Josie is a junior at Oakdale, is that right, Josie?"

Josie nods. Katie-Rose bounces in her seat, because her favorite babysitter in the world goes to Oakdale High School. Her name is Chrissy, and she's a freshman, and she does things like paint her fingernails bright orange. In fact, she's the perfect example of how to grow up without growing up, and Katie-Rose wants to be just like her when she's in high school. Last weekend Chrissy dyed her blond hair "vampire red," and supposedly her mom had a cow.

"Hi," Josie says, waving at the class.

Katie-Rose beams and waves back. She wonders if Josie and Chrissy know each other.

"Well, from what I heard, I think your teacher pretty much explained everything," Josie says. She holds up the stack of papers. "The information slips are right here, so if you want to take the class, write down your name, your parents' names, and your telephone number. Tear that part off and leave it with your teacher. The top part has all the details about class safety and what my credentials are and stuff like that, so take that part home and show your parents."

She takes roughly half of the papers and hands them to Chance, who passes them backward over his head without taking one.

Katie-Rose is flabbergasted that anyone would pass up the opportunity to learn how to do tricks on the trapeze. But Chance is obnoxious, and she doesn't want him in the trapeze class anyway. All he would do is ruin it.

"The first class is this Thursday, so I'll come back this afternoon and collect the names of everyone who's interested," Josie says. "Then, over the next couple of days, I'll call everyone's parents to reassure them that I won't let you die or break your arm or anything."

Kids laugh. They like Josie already, as does Katie-Rose.

"Anyway, once your parents give me their permission for you to be in the class, you're good to go," Josie finishes. "Cool?"

Very, Katie-Rose thinks. Because . . . trapeze lessons! Trapeze lessons are exactly what fifth grade is all about— or what it *should* be about. Not sick moms or mean girls or gross boys.

No. Fifth grade is about FUN: Friends Until Near-death. Actually, friends until full-fledged death, not just near-death. Not that she wants to die. But then the letters would spell "fuffd," and what the heck-a-doodle is fuffd? She drums her fingers on her desk. *Fuffd. Fuh-fuh-duh. Fuh-fuh-duh, fuh-fuh-duh, fuh-fuh-duh.*

Ooo! She's got it! FUFFD means Fools Under False Feebleminded Delusions. And what sort of delusions? Delusions about . . . growing up, Katie-Rose concludes. About needing to be "mature," when it is *so* not time for the FFFs to be mature. Fifth grade—to steal Chuck E. Cheese's slogan—is where a kid can be a kid, and trapezes are the absolute definition of kids being kids.

She leans toward Yasaman and whispers, "Yaz, we *have* to sign up! Okay? Okay. Good!"

"I wish," Yasaman whispers back.

"What do you mean, you wish? You can't go through life wishing. You have to act!" She thumps Yasaman on the back. "So it's settled. Yay!"

"Ow," Yasaman says. "And, yes, it *is* settled, you're right. Just not in the way you mean. Do you honestly think my parents would let me take trapeze lessons?"

"Why not?"

Yasaman doesn't answer. She fingers her *hijab*, and Katie-Rose wonders if it has to do with being Muslim. Are Muslims not allowed to do trapeze tricks? Are Muslim *girls* not allowed to do trapeze tricks? Katie-Rose has gotten vague glimpses, through her friendship with Yaz, of a world in which some Muslim girls aren't supposed to do certain things with boys, whether the boys are Muslim are not. *But Yaz is in school with boys. Der.* So why would trapeze lessons be any different?

At the front of the room, Josie rocks back and forth on the balls of her feet. "So I'm super psyched to work with you guys," she says. "And it's fine if you don't have any experience or whatever."

"What if you're a spaz?" Preston calls out. "What if you

have super bad aim, and when you throw your fruit away, it hits someone's head?"

The plum, Katie-Rose thinks, growing warm. Josie wouldn't turn down a girl for accidentally lobbing a plum at someone's head, would she?

"No fruit throwing," Josie says. "But if you're worried about your motor skills, don't be. Learning trapeze is a great way to improve your coordination."

"Hear that, Katie-Rose?" Preston says. "You should join!"

Modessa snorts. "Good one, Preston." She kicks the leg of Elena's chair, and Elena jumps.

"Right," Elena says. "*Ha*. Ha ha ha."

Oh, shut up, Katie-Rose thinks, because she could care less what Medusa, Preston, and "ha ha ha" Elena think. She *is* going to sign up. She'll make sure Milla signs up, too, and since Violet's absent, she'll grab a spare information slip for her as well.

Josie turns to Ms. Perez. "I guess that's all." She holds the remaining info sheets against her chest. "Um, can you tell me how to get to the other fifth-grade classroom?"

"Sure," Ms. Perez says. "Just go back into the hall, take a left, and pass the two preschool rooms. You won't be able to miss them. They're doing a dinosaur unit, and dinosaurs are *all* over the wall. When you get to the water fountain, take a sharp right. Mr. Emerson's class will be the second room you come to."

Yasaman surprises Katie-Rose by jabbing her hand into the air.

"You should walk her to Mr. Emerson's room yourself," Yaz says without waiting for Ms. Perez to call on her. "It's pretty confusing."

"Are you nuts?" Katie-Rose says. "No, it's not."

There's a flurry of movement, and a stabbing pain makes Katie-Rose's eyes water. *What the . . . ?* She looks down to see Yasaman's jeans-clad leg jutting out at a sharp sideways angle, bridging the gap between Yasaman's desk and her own. Yasaman's black Converse is mere inches from Katie-Rose's beat-up sneaker with its untied laces, and Katie-Rose puts the pieces together. Yasaman, for utterly no reason, just stomped on her toes!

"Hey!" she protests.

Yasaman does it again, and this time she keeps her foot planted on top of Katie-Rose's, applying firm and steady pressure.

"It might not be confusing to *you*," Yaz says to Katie-Rose, only without actually looking at Katie-Rose. Her gaze, both earnest and innocent, stays on Ms. Perez. "But Josie hasn't gone to school here for seven years."

"True," Ms. Perez says.

"I just think it would be the polite thing to do," Yaz says.

Ms. Perez blinks. "Oh. I suppose . . . I suppose you're right, Yasaman. Josie, would you like me to show you the way?"

"I'll take her," Chance volunteers, and because he's Chance, Katie-Rose knows that he just wants an excuse to leave class.

"*No*," Yaz says. "It has to be Ms. Perez."

Katie-Rose eyes her friend. She wiggles her toes within her sneaker. Yasaman's foot grinds down.

"Why?" Chance says.

Yasaman swallows. "Because . . . because . . ."

"Because it's a teacher's job to escort visitors," Katie-Rose tells him. She doesn't know what Yaz is up to, but it doesn't matter. "It says so in the Rivendell handbook."

"Right," Yasaman says. She slides her foot off of

Katie-Rose's. If she, too, knows there's no such thing as a Rivendell handbook, she doesn't let on.

"Well, all right, then," Ms. Perez says. "I'm more than happy to be your escort, Josie."

"Um, okay, but I'm sure I could find the way on my own," Josie says.

"No, no, don't be silly," Ms. Perez says. She gives a small laugh. "It's no problem at all, really." She straightens her skirt and adjusts her blouse, and it seems to Katie-Rose as if she's primping, which is just plain weird.

Or then again, maybe it's not. As Ms. Perez leads Josie out of the room, the back of Katie-Rose's neck tingles. There was a time not long ago when Yasaman was stuck on the idea that the FFFs should set Ms. Perez and Mr. Emerson up. Like, as a couple.

The idea faded, but now it seems to have resurfaced, at least in Yasaman's earnest, foot-stomping soul.

Is this a sign of the bras-and-lipstick sort of changes that Katie-Rose fears? She'll follow up on this with Yasaman later, that's for sure.

But right now there are more pressing concerns at

hand. The information sheets have reached Ava, who sits in front of Katie-Rose. Unlike Chance, Ava *does* take one. Then she lifts the rest above her head and wiggles them.

Katie-Rose grabs them and slides two sheets from the stack: One for herself, and one for Violet. Then, acting on instinct, she takes a third, because sometimes it takes an outsider to see what's best for a person.

Plus, she really thinks it's unlikely that taking trapeze lessons is against the rules of Islam. Why would it be? Why would Allah—who to Katie-Rose seems pretty much like God, only Muslim—care?

Yasaman Tercan, she writes on the top sheet of her small stack. She knows Yasaman's parents' names, and of course she knows Yaz's telephone number, so she writes all of that down, too. *Easy-peasy*. Next she fills out Violet's sheet, and last of all, hers.

With a frown, she chews on the eraser of her pencil. Should she have snagged a sheet for Milla, too? *Nah*, she tells herself. Milla's no dummy. She's sure to have grasped the epic appeal of trapeze lessons all on her own.

Yaz and Violet will ultimately get on board, too, of course, and she'll be queenly and gracious when they thank her. They'll be like, "You already filled out the boring paperwork for us, Katie-Rose? But when? Where? How did you know we needed you to?"

"Oh, don't be silly," she'll say breezily. "Friends know what's best for each other, and honestly I was happy to do it. Yes, I'm just that awesome."

four

Violet

*V*iolet hears the phone ring, but she ignores it. Her dad, who came home early, is in the kitchen getting dinner ready, and Violet is sitting with her mom in the TV room, the two of them sharing the big purple armchair. Yes, the chair is meant for one person, and yes, Violet is squished, especially since she made a point of contorting her own body in order to leave her mom the most room possible. But the squishiness doesn't matter, not one bit. That's how glad Violet is to have her mom back.

Another gladness? Her mom *smells* like her mom again. In the hospital (the, um, mental hospital, though Violet prefers to delete that first part), her mom smelled weird. Not *awful*, but not good. It was as if the real smell of her still existed, but deep deep down, practically buried by the scent of hand sanitizer and hospital air.

The idea of being buried is not a happy thought, and Violet shoos it from her mind. *Good-bye, bad thought*, she says silently, just the way her therapist taught her.

"Don't make a big deal out of what you consider to be 'bad thoughts,'" Dr. Altebrando encouraged Violet back in Atlanta. It was two weeks after her mom had her breakdown.

"Just acknowledge the bad thoughts, no more and no less. If you fight them, they'll fight back, pushing harder to get in. But if you allow them to pass on through"—Dr. Altebrando splayed her fingers and smiled gently—"they'll get the message."

"When?" Violet asked.

"Eventually. It will take time, but they *will* stop coming around."

Dr. Altebrando promised she was telling the truth, so Violet tried to take her advice. Months later, she's still trying. Is it getting easier? She thinks so . . . but having her mom back home again, while awesome, is also surprisingly stressful.

She doesn't want anything to go wrong. She, Violet, doesn't want to *do* anything wrong.

"Boo?" her dad says. In one hand is his Coke, and in the other is the phone, which he jiggles in front of her. "It's for you. Didn't you hear me calling?"

Violet hesitates, reluctant to interrupt this moment with her mom. But—*oh no*. Her mom misreads the situation and rises from the chair.

"I'll just give you some privacy," she says. "Girls your age need their privacy, I certainly do know that."

Violet tugs at her.

"Mom, wait. You still have more songs to hear." That's what they've been doing, snuggled up in the purple chair. Violet's playing songs for her mom on her iPod, introducing her to new artists and bands she thinks her mom will like. One aftereffect of her mom's extended . . . *absence . . .*

is that she's fallen behind on all sorts of stuff. Music is just one example.

Violet's mom sinks back down, but her dad is still standing before her with the phone, so *fine*. She takes it. Her dad plants a quick kiss on her head, and another on the top of Violet's mom's head, then disappears back into the kitchen.

"Hello?" Violet says into the phone.

"HI!" Katie-Rose says, her voice big and loud. "GUESS WHAT? I'M WITH MILLA AND YAZ! WE'RE IN MILLA'S MOM'S VAN, AND GUESS WHERE WE ARE?"

Violet switches the phone to her outside ear, the one farthest from her mom. "Um, getting a ride home from school? Listen, you're kind of yelling. You're kind of bursting my eardrum, Katie-Rose."

"Oh. Sorry," Katie-Rose says, taking it down a few notches. "We are on the way home from school, but Mrs. Swanson isn't dropping us off at our *own* homes. Yet. We're, like, five blocks from your house! Isn't that awesometatiousful?"

Awesometatiousful is a word Katie-Rose made up, and it means exactly what it sounds like: when something is even more full of awesomeness, and tatiousness, than the regular garden variety of "awesome."

Violet's heart beats faster. "Why?"

"Why what? Why is it awesometatiousful?!" Katie-Rose huffs. "Why do you have to ask, you silly potato?"

"No," Violet says, sensing her mom watching her. "What I mean is, why are you . . . you know . . . what you just said?"

"Huh?"

"Forget it."

"You weren't at school, and we missed you," Katie-Rose scolds. "Why weren't you, by the way? Are you sick?"

"No, I just wanted to stay with my mom. Just for today."

"Ahh," Katie-Rose says. "Thought so." To the others, but also to Violet, since Violet's ear is right there waiting to be bursted some more, Katie-Rose bellows, "I was right! She just wanted time with her mom!"

It sounds so simple when Katie-Rose says it. Like it makes sense, even, so Violet doesn't explain how hard she had to fight to get her dad to let her, or how worried she was about her mom being alone. Like, what if her mother wasn't able to find the cereal? Or if the hot water ran out like it does sometimes?

"Violet, your mother is an adult," her dad said. "She knows how to fix breakfast for herself."

"But—"

"Sweetie, she can take care of herself. She really can. She took care of you for years and years, now, didn't she?"

His sentence hung there. It just ... hung there, and the look on her dad's face was one Violet never wants to see again.

"I totally understand," Katie-Rose says to Violet, bringing her back. "You wanted to be there for her."

"Yes," Violet says. How nice it is to be understood— and really, does she need to give Katie-Rose *all* the details?

"You wanted to be with her just like *we* want to be there for *you*! Yay! So we can meet your mom! Double-yay!"

"Wait—what?" Violet presses the phone hard against her ear. She shrinks into the purple chair, curving her body into a C.

"... so I said, 'Oh, it's *fine*. Why wouldn't she want to see us, her best friends in the world?' I mean, right?"

Violet opens her mouth. Nothing comes out.

"Yoo-hoo!" Katie-Rose says. "It's your turn to talk now, Violet!"

"Katie-Rose, give me a sec," Violet says. Katie-Rose *is* right that the four flower friends are, and always will be, the best of besties. It's just that Violet thought Katie-Rose understood how she was feeling, but she doesn't, and now Violet feels bowled over. Sometimes Katie-Rose can be like a steamroller, relentlessly moving forward regardless of what she has to run over to get there. A cheerful steamroller, the sort that would grin at toddlers from the pages of a picture book filled with honks and loud noises, but a steamroller nonetheless.

"Katie-Rose, you're smothering her," says a farther-away voice. It's Milla. Violet hears rustling, and then an indignant "*Hey!*" from Katie-Rose, and then Milla is on the line.

"Hi, Violet," Milla says. "How *are* you?"

"I'm good," Violet says. "I'm, uh, really good."

"Oh, *good!*" Milla exclaims.

It's a lot of "goods" all at once. Both girls giggle.

"Tell her 'hi' for me," Yasaman chimes in. She's sitting next to Milla, probably. Or no, she'd be sitting in the back seat of Milla's mom's van along with Katie-Rose, and Milla would be in the front passenger seat. Violet can see her friends in her mind, and it makes her heart ache.

"Yaz says 'hi,' too," Milla says. "We're all super excited to meet your mom. Is it *so* great, having her back home?"

Violet nods. Then, remembering that nods are silent, she clears her throat. "It is. Yes. Totally. How are *you*?"

"I'm fabulous, thanks for asking," Katie-Rose says, who apparently yanked back the phone. "I'll be even *more* fabulous—haha, impossible, I know—once we get to your house. We'll be there in two minutes, 'kay?"

"No!" Violet cries.

Her mom flinches, and Violet sucks in a deep breath. Violet's mother is not to be startled. Violet's mother is not to be disturbed in any way.

She exhales. She breathes in and out again for good measure. When she's pretty sure she's reined in her emotions, she says, "What I mean is, not today, but thanks so much for asking. Rain check?"

Violet's mom taps her. "Who is it, Boo? Is it one of your friends? Does she want to have a playdate?"

Playdate? Did her mom just say *playdate?* Violet is ten. Ten-year-olds don't have "playdates." *Does her mother not know her anymore?*

"You should go, baby," Violet's mom continues. "Goodness, don't stay home because of me."

"I heard your mom's voice!" Katie-Rose squeals, her excitement suggesting that she just spotted a woodland fawn or an endangered dolphin. "What'd she say?"

Violet presses the entire phone to her chest, smothering the listening part *and* the talking-into part. "It's Katie-Rose," she tells her mom. She scrambles for a plausible lie. "She, um, wants to practice mental telepathy. We do that sometimes. You know, to see if we can send messages to each other using our minds?"

Violet's mom pulls her eyebrows together.

"It's fun!" Violet says, too cheerily. "It's just that right now isn't the best time, because . . . because it doesn't work if you're in the middle of something else. Which I am, because you and I are hanging out and listening to music and . . . yeah." She makes herself hush, afraid of overselling it. She and Katie-Rose have never practiced ESP together. They've never even tried.

She brings the phone back to her ear. "So another time. Okay, Katie-Rose?"

"But we have a present for you!" Katie-Rose says. "It's more for your mom, but you'll like it, too. It's a butterfly bush!"

"A . . . *what?*" Violet says. "Never mind. But thanks! But, would one of you hold on to it for me for now? Okay, that's awesome. Great. Bye!"

She presses the phone's off button. She slips her thumb to the side of the phone and turns the whole thing off, ringer and all. She leans forward and puts it on the coffee table, giving it a shove so that it slides out of reach.

She smiles at her mom even though she feels as if a giant hand is pushing on her, and she's going under.

Do not go under, she commands herself. *You have to be strong. You are the strong one, and it's your job to keep your mom from going under.*

She picks up her abandoned iPod and scrolls through playlists. Music is like poetry, and her mom loves poetry. Poems mixed with melodies will keep them both afloat.

A title catches her eye. *Yes.* She hits the play button, and the opening chords twine around them.

Her mom strokes Violet's head. "Oh, I like this," she murmurs. "So pretty. What's it called?"

"'Defying Gravity,'" Violet tells her. "I like it, too."

Tuesday, October 18

Yasaman

Um . . . hi! The Big Begonia page is for public service announcements, right? Well, I know it is waaay early and none of y'all are going to see this right away, cuz either you're hitting the snooze button again and again on your alarm (KATIE-ROSE) or eating a delicious homemade scone (MILLA) or—hopefully—just, you know, getting ready for school (VIOLET).

 Yasaman

I mean, cuz since it's a school day and that's what kids do on school days.

 Yasaman

Did that come out weird? If it did, I am SO sorry. I just miss you, Violet. Rivendell isn't the same without you!!!! Oh, and speaking of Rivendell, we have a *situation* to fill you in on. A yucky and shocking situation concerning Modessa and ELENA, of all people, and it's not what you think, either. It's not, "Oh, no! Modessa is bullying someone again, and that someone is Elena!" In fact, it's the opposite. Modessa and Quin are teaching Elena to be a bully *with* them, if you can believe it.

Yasaman

Katie-Rose put it best, I think. She said Elena's their new *recruit*, and if you're as shocked as I am, well, then I know how you feel. It makes my skin crawl, that's how shocked I am. *shudders*

 Yasaman

But that's not the announcement I got online to make. My *real* Big Begonia announcement is about the butterfly bush Milla's mom got for your mom. I'm the one who took it home yesterday—Milla was very nice and let me be the one to plant-sit it—and omigosh, I love it sooooooo much!

 Yasaman

I put it in our backyard so it wld have fresh air, and last night I sat with it for like an hour so it wouldn't be lonely. BUT DON'T WORRY! I KNOW IT'S YOURS! Or your mom's. Whatever.

 Yasaman

Mainly I just wanted to tell you how beautiful it is, since you haven't seen it yet. It's bursting with purple blossoms, and it smells incredible. No wonder butterflies 🖤 it!

Yasaman

Wldn't it be amazing to be a butterfly? Wldn't it be amazing to be able to fly, period? Not in an airplane, or with fairy wings, or with any sort of *wing* wings, which rules out being a butterfly, I guess.

 Yasaman

What I mean is—

 Yasaman

Urghh.

 Yasaman

I don't know if I can explain it, but sometimes I just . . .

 Yasaman

I wish I cld be *more* than myself, in a floating-through-white-puffy-clouds sort of way. I wish my soul could swoop out of my body and soar into the sky, and while I was up there, I cld look around and see *everything*. Do any of you ever daydream about things like that? And wish you weren't trapped in your own life for a while?

 Yasaman

Not that I don't love my life! I *totally* do. I love Nigar, who thinks she's such a big girl since she's turning 4 next month. I love that she wants to have a bubblegum party, cuz what IS a bubblegum party, even? She wants to be Princess Bubbles, that's as far as we've gotten in terms of party planning.

Yasaman

I also love my mom, who smoothed oil into my hair after my bath last night. (And if you're wondering *why* she smoothed oil into my hair, it's because that is the top-sekrit secret to having shiny hair. Now you know, Milla, since you're always asking. If you want, I'll ask if she'll do your hair one day. I'm sure she would. The oil is scented with roses, yum!)

Yasaman

And also I love my *baba*, and one reason out of many is because he let me take the Web Spinners class at the Muslim Youth Center last summer, remember? If I hadn't taken that class, then I wouldn't be a "computer genius" (K-R's words, not mine!). And if I wasn't a computer genius, we wouldn't have our special flower power website with coolio features like . . . well . . . the Big Begonia! Where I get to leave messages for YOU PEOPLE, my BFF/FFFs!!! 🩶 🩶

 Yasaman

As someone who once had **ZERO** friends, believe me when I say that I will ALWAYS love you and never stop, not today and not 65 years from today, when we're 75 and playing old lady games like bunko, which my *büyükanne* plays every Wednesday with her old-lady friends.

 Yasaman

That will rock, being old-lady friends together. Except now I can't remember why I logged on in the 1st place. I know I had a public service announcement . . .

Yasaman

Oh! Right!

Yasaman

Um . . . they came! The butterflies!!!! Not last night, cuz it was nighttime. Der. But this morning I woke up with the strangest feeling that something special was going to happen. I didn't know what, just that it was going to be special.

Yasaman

Of course right as I was lying in bed thinking about it, Nigar came running into my room, wanting me to fix her hair. And of course when I started brushing it, she changed her mind, because of the tangles. Of course.

 Yasaman

She squirmed away and went over to my dresser, and I was like, "Nigar, leave my stuff alone." So she skipped to the window and looked out at the backyard and said, "Yaz! Come see!"

 Yasaman

So I did, and they were there! Real, live s!

 Yasaman

There was an orange one, a yellow one, a bluish-green one, and a speckled brown one with gold at the edge of its wings. That makes *four*—did everyone catch that? *Four* butterflies, all fluttering around the butterfly bush in its big pot, and don't make fun of me, but . . . I think it's a sign. I think the butterflies came to my house for a reason, and the reason was to remind me how beautiful life is.

Yasaman

Not everything is beautiful, maybe. But there's more good in the world than bad. I really believe that, just like I believe it's our job to add to the world's goodness. By using our flower power! Like we promised we wld back when we first became flower friends!

 Yasaman

Soooooooooooooooo . . .

 Yasaman

I've given it some thought—LOTS of thought—and I think we need to get serious about setting up Mr. Emerson and Ms. Perez!!!!! We *said* we were going to ages ago, after all. Plus, who better to plant the seed of love—*seed* of love, get it?—than four fabulous flowers?

 Yasaman

Is everyone up for Plan Teacherly Love? Plz say yes!!!! And now good-bye! Peace, butterflies, and flower power FOREVER!!!!

❈ five ❈

Violet

There are butterflies in Violet's stomach. Actually, no. The butterflies aren't in her stomach. They're in her rib cage, and they're frantic and edgy, flapping their wings against her ribs. They're making her heart beat way too fast.

"Are you sure, Boo?" her mother asks. A wrinkle forms in the middle of her forehead. "It makes more sense, and your dad could get to work earlier. And I want to see your school and meet your friends."

"No, Dad always takes me," Violet says. "He doesn't mind, do you, Dad?"

Violet's dad spreads his hands. The car keys are already in one of them. "I'm fine with whatever, but we do need to get going."

"Then let's go already," Violet says. "*I'm* not the one being slow." She hears in her voice that she's being bratty. *Imperious,* her dad would normally say, but nothing's normal, so for once he doesn't call her on it.

Violet's mom opens her mouth as if *she's* going to scold Violet, but then she closes it. Violet can hardly stand it. Yesterday, Violet couldn't bear to leave the house. Today, she can't bear to stay a moment longer, so she grabs her lunch from the counter—the lunch her mom packed, which Violet had to *re*pack, which is what started the day's badness—and bangs out the back door.

"Bye, baby," her mom calls.

Violet presses her lips together and strides across the driveway to get to the garage, which is twenty feet or so behind the house. In Atlanta, their house had an attached garage. In Atlanta, their favorite place to get chicken nuggets was Chick-fil-A, who never served them up raw.

Violet hears a kiss—her dad pecking her mom's cheek,

probably—and then his deep voice saying, "Call if you need *any*thing. I can be home in fifteen minutes. All right?"

Her mom forces a laugh. "Please, you two. I'm sorry about the chicken. It was a silly mistake, and I'm sorry. Will you stop worrying?"

"Lavinia ...," her dad says.

Violet gets into the front seat of the Range Rover and closes the door, craving silence. She holds her lunch in her lap. She knows she won't eat any of it, even though there's nothing wrong with it anymore. She'll throw it away before school starts. Even so, she can't help imagining what would have happened if she hadn't noticed the box of frozen chicken nuggets on the granite island.

She *didn't*, not right away. What she noticed, when she first came downstairs, was her mom, humming as she bustled around the kitchen.

"Mom, you're up," Violet said, surprise blooming inside her.

"Well, of course, Boo," her mom said. "I've already packed your lunch—"

"You *have?*" It wasn't all that long ago that packing Violet's lunch, or simply thinking about packing Violet's lunch, would have thrown Violet's mom into a tailspin of worry, because one task led to another and another, *and it was all too much.*

"And now I'm going to fix you breakfast. How does oatmeal sound?"

"Um, oatmeal sounds great." Violet couldn't stop smiling. "Thanks, Mom."

"With plenty of butter and brown sugar, just the way you like it," her mom announced. She returned Violet's smile. "And you are very welcome."

With no lunch to pack and no breakfast to prepare, Violet felt at a loss. Then she saw the chicken nugget box lying on the counter. She went to it, thinking she could help clean up, and out of habit, she skimmed the description of the breaded chicken nuggets within.

"Mom?" she said.

"What, baby? What do you need?"

Violet bit her lip. Maybe she was jumping to conclusions. *Surely* she was jumping to conclusions, so before saying anything more, she would simply check. Was the oven on? She checked the display, and no, it wasn't. But it could have been on before Violet came downstairs, right?

Because *der*, her mom would have turned it off when she took the chicken nuggets out.

She sidled up beside her mom, who was using the stove to boil water for her oatmeal. She placed her hand on the oven's glass door. It was cool to the touch, and a knot formed in her gut.

She grabbed the insulated lunch bag sitting on the counter. The Velcro strip at the top made a rough, ugly sound as she pulled it open.

"Chicken nuggets, grapes, string cheese, and two Oreos," her mom recited. "Sound good?"

Violet felt around in the lunch bag. Her fingers grazed the bag of grapes, and she thought of Halloween, and eyeballs-that-weren't-eyeballs at haunted houses. From there, she thought of intestines that weren't intestines, just cold spaghetti noodles. Cold, but still *cooked*, or else they'd be the texture of pick-up sticks, which wouldn't do at all.

She found the chicken nuggets, and her throat constricted. They were icy and hard. By the time lunch rolled around, they would have thawed, and if Violet had popped one into her mouth, her teeth would have cut past the breading into pink, slippery flesh. Dead, but uncooked. *Raw.*

She would have spit it out, and everyone would have looked her way. The scene played out in her mind:

Katie-Rose, loving the gross-out factor, would be delighted. *Your mom packed you raw chicken? Awesome sauce!*

Milla's mouth would fall open, and then she'd remember her manners and fix her expression. *Katie-Rose, no,* she'd say. *Raw chicken is really dangerous.*

Natalia would jump in, saying, *It ith. It hath thalmonella, and thalmonella can kill you, Katie-Rothe.*

But Yasaman's reaction would have been the worst. *Everybody, hush,* she'd say. She'd search Violet's face, and Violet would want to die. *Violet? Are you okay? Do you want me to take you to the office?*

Violet pulled the chicken nuggets out of her lunch bag. Her insides trembled.

"Boo?" her mom said, puzzled.

Violet threw the raw chicken nuggets in the trash. Not trusting herself to speak, she picked up the cardboard box they came in and handed it to her mom.

Nuggets are UNCOOKED, it said in big bold letters. *For safety, this product must be cooked to an internal temperature of 170°F as measured by use of a meat thermometer. Cooking times may vary.*

The directions weren't hidden, or in a foreign language, or able to be seen only with special glasses. If a ten-year-old could figure it out, why couldn't a grown woman?

Her dad walks toward the car. Violet sees him in the side mirror. Her mom stays by the house, her hand to her mouth. Violet bets she's chewing her nails. Back in Atlanta, her mom used to chew her nails all the way past the white part, exposing the tender tips of her fingers. Then she'd be stuck with no nails. No fingernails for scratching Violet's back, no fingernails for picking bits of lint off her father's suit jacket, no fingernails for coaxing her own zipper up when the metal tab got wedged down too far.

Sometimes Violet had to zip up her mom's jeans for her. *That is so wrong*, Violet thinks, shifting her gaze to the SUV's glove compartment. It's made out of some sort of hard plastic. It's beige, and it's blurry. It's not usually blurry.

Her dad climbs into the driver's seat and shuts the door.

"Finally," Violet mutters.

His head snaps sideways.

"What?" Violet demands.

He sets his jaw and reverses out of the garage. Violet's mom is still standing at the back door of the house, and she comes in and out of Violet's sight line as her father executes a flawless three-point turn. When the Range Rover faces forward, so does Violet, separated from her mother only by the shatterproof windshield.

Her mom stops chewing her nails in order to wave good-bye. Her expression—both hopeful and woebegone—transforms Violet's anger into shame.

She hurt her mother, who needs to be protected.

She made her mom feel like she can't do stuff. Like she's dumb, or helpless, or . . . unwell. Violet's heart hammers in her chest, because what if her mom *is* unwell, and everyone's just pretending she isn't, and she has to go back to the hospital and not be at home anymore? Not be better???

Violet wants to make her father stop the car. She wants

to run back to her mom and hug her. But her dad honks as he peels out of the driveway, and it startles her, and before she knows it, they're driving away from the house.

It's too late to say, "No, please don't! Go back!"

It's too late to even say good-bye.

Six

Camilla

O n Tuesday morning. Milla arrives at Rivendell at her usual, somewhat early time. She walks
down the hall toward Mr. Emerson's room, just like
yesterday, and just like yesterday, she turns the corner
and almost collides with Modessa, Quin, and Elena.
Unlike yesterday, there are other kids in the hall this
time, but they part on instinct to give Modessa and her
companions room. They scoot out of the way because the
three girls are evil. Indeed, they proclaim their evilness
with matching shirts; well, matching in that Modessa's

says Evil Chick #1, Quin's says Evil Chick #2, and Elena's says Evil Chick #3. Their arms are linked. Their smiles are smug.

Milla almost turns tail and scurries in the other direction. That's what her body wants her to do. *But she isn't that Milla anymore*, so she doesn't. Also, there's Elena to think of. Elena who loves animals, a fact that suggests she loves chickens, a fact that suggests she doesn't think chickens are evil.

Yet here she is, passing herself off as evil chick number three to Modessa's evil chick number one. It isn't right.

The three evil chicks draw closer. Milla's palms get sweaty, because she knows she has to do something. She didn't do anything when *she* was under Modessa's wing, and that knowledge haunts her.

Katie-Rose, Yaz, and Violet are the ones who saved her, and she'll always be grateful. Now, as a way to act on that gratitude, it's Milla's time to return the favor. Elena needs Milla's help whether she realizes it or not.

"Hi, Elena," she says right before their paths cross.

"H-hi, Milla," Elena says. She looks at Modessa, who gives a tiny, disgusted shake of her head. She's too disappointed to expend more than the barest minimum of energy on correcting Elena. That's the message Modessa seems to want to convey.

"Nice shirt," Milla says.

Elena smiles, then doesn't smile, then smiles again, but timidly. "Really? You don't think we'll get in trouble for wearing them?"

"Elena?" Modessa says, both condescending and put-out. "Camilla is lying to you. She doesn't like your shirt. Or she thinks she doesn't. Really, she's just jealous."

Oh, that tone. That tone brings back so many memories, all of them unpleasant.

Milla? There's food in your teeth. It's gross.

Milla? I'm sure you were trying to be nice by loaning your pencil to Ava, but don't do that again. If you let people treat you like a doormat, they'll keep treating you like, well, a doormat.

Milla? Please don't make that sound when you swallow. No offense, but it makes me vomit a little in my throat.

Milla tried for days—for weeks—to figure out what sound she made when she swallowed. Modessa could hear it, and so could Quin, since she said it made her want to vomit, too, but not Milla. So she just stopped eating . . . until Modessa told her not to do that, either.

Milla? she said in that awful tone of fake and weary concern. *Having an eating disorder is, like, embarrassing. Also? No offense? But you're already too skinny, as in bad skinny. You do want to have boobs one day, don't you?*

Milla shakes her head, and she shakes it *hard*, nothing like Modessa's slight shake of disdain. She shakes those memories out of her head and flings them far, far away.

"Okay, I don't like your shirt," she confesses to Elena, whose face falls.

Modessa snorts. "See?"

"I mean, it's *good* for what it is," Milla says, "and I think it's cool that you all made shirts together—"

"*Do you*, Milla?" Modessa says.

"Yeah," Quin says. "*Do* you?"

She doesn't. She thinks the concept of friends making

shirts together is cool, but fine, her opinion doesn't apply to Modessa, Elena, and Quin, because she doesn't think they *are* friends. Not real friends.

"But, um, you *might* get in trouble," Milla says. "I don't know. Like if Ms. Westerfeld thought you were pretending to be witches . . . ?"

"Now why in the world would we do that?" Modessa asks. She regards Milla pityingly. "We *are* witches, silly." She turns to Elena. "Poor Camilla. For a while, I thought maybe, *maybe*, she had what it took."

Back her eyes slide to Milla. They are stained glass: shiny and glittering, but with nothing behind them. "But you don't, do you, Milla? You just don't have what it takes, and you turned out to be so easily replaced."

Modessa puts her arm around Elena. The gesture is a challenge. It says, *She is mine. Once, you were mine. Don't you know that whatever I want, I get?*

Milla is officially creeped out, especially by the "witches" part. Modessa knows Milla is superstitious. She knows Milla is afraid of the dark, and all it represents.

She holds it together, though, because Modessa is

glossing over an extremely important point. Modessa doesn't always get what she wants. Milla left her, not the other way around.

"Um, you could switch into a Rivendell shirt," Milla suggests to Elena. "You can buy one from Mr. McGreevy, and he'll put it on your parents' account."

Elena swallows. Does *she* make a sound when she does? If so, it eludes Milla entirely.

Milla holds out her hand, palm up. "Come on. I'll walk you to the office."

"No," Modessa says, no longer sickly-sweet. Her expression hardens, and she steps between Milla and Elena. She places her hands on Elena's shoulders and says, "You don't talk to Camilla, for your own good. You can smile at Camilla, but that's all. And only like this." She bares her teeth at Milla and *growls*, making Milla jump.

Modessa laughs. She growls again, and Quin growls with her. Quin jabs Elena, and Elena joins in. Once she gives herself over to it, she really gives herself over to it, peeling her lips away from her teeth and adding a menacing hiss.

Milla's pulse races. It's awful how they transform

themselves, and it's especially awful in Elena's case. They are a pack of wild wolf-girls, and Elena, as a wolf-girl, is no longer timid or confused. While Modessa's eyes are made of stained glass, Elena's are dark pits.

It's as if Modessa really has cast a spell on her. As if she is a witch. Milla knows in her head how ridiculous that is, but her heart says otherwise and tries to jump out of her skin as she hurries past them.

Instead of going to Mr. Emerson's class, she flees to the girls' bathroom and locks herself in a stall for a full five minutes. When she emerges, she looks at herself in the mirror and sees a coward. Her face is drained of color. *Her* eyes are big, blue, and stupid.

Later, sitting in Mr. Emerson's classroom, she calms down. She tells herself again how silly Modessa and Quin and Elena are, pretending to be witches or wolf-girls or vampires, for all she knows. It does seem as though they've shed their "girl" identities, though. But if they're not girls, what are they? Or if they are girls, but they're also something else, what are they? What do you call a girl who bares her teeth and growls? What do you call a girl with black pits for eyes?

She doesn't know. She's not good with words. Violet, who writes poetry and posts it on LuvYaBunches.com, is excellent with words, and if Milla asked her to, she's sure Violet could come up with the perfect term for girls who are both more than and less than real girls.

Milla doesn't want to bother her, though. When Violet came into Mr. Emerson's room soon after Milla, Milla hopped up and gave her the biggest hug ever, hoping to give strength to Violet and receive strength from Violet simultaneously. Violet hugged her back, but pulled away quickly. Milla doesn't think they got much of anything from each other, which was sad.

"So, children of the corn, is everyone clear on how to divide one fraction by another?" Mr. Emerson asks. Milla blinks. She has no clue how to divide one fraction by another, just as she has no clue why Mr. Emerson sometimes calls them "children of the corn." But does it matter? She craves the freedom of morning break, so she adds her "yes" to the chorus of everyone else's.

"*Riiight*," Mr. Emerson says. "Sure you do." He waves his arm toward the door. "Go on, then! Play, frolic, and run wildly about like the savages you are!"

Milla joins the others as they head for the door. She and Violet are separated in all the jostling, and the October wind whips her hair around her face. It makes her feel bold—not witchy bold, but Milla bold—and she's almost able to forget the pale, big-eyed coward in the girls' room mirror. She pulls a hair elastic off her wrist and secures her hair in a ponytail.

"Max!" she calls, spotting him with his best friend, Thomas.

He glances over his shoulder, and she jogs over. The wind is having fun with his thick hair, fluffing it into even more of a puffball than usual.

"Hi," she says. She takes a sec to catch her breath, and to figure out why she's there in the first place. Because Max is so solid? Because Max, if Milla asked him about witches, would quote some Discovery Channel show like *Mythbusters* and tell her—in detail—why witches don't and can't exist?

"Can I, um, talk to you?" she says.

"Sure," Max answers.

They stand there, Max and Milla and Thomas. Max and Milla look at each other. Then they look at Thomas.

"Really?" Thomas says. He spreads his hands to say, *Dude, you're casting me aside for a girl?*

"I just need him for a few minutes, and then you can have him back," Milla says. "Oh. And, um, hi, Thomas."

Thomas narrows his eyes. "Mmm-hmm. *Hellooooo,* Milla."

Milla knows his attitude is just for show. She likes Thomas. He's a rascal—that's what her Mom Abigail would call him—but he doesn't insult people or be mean just for the fun of it like some of the fifth-grade boys.

(Or like some of the fifth-grade girls. Wolf-girls. Witchy girls.)

Shush, Milla tells herself. This is not the time to think about that. There is no reason to think about Modessa when she is with cute, sweet, puffbally Max.

"We could go over by the fence," Max suggests.

"Yeah, good idea," she says.

The fence is long and circles the entire playground, so as long as they pick an unoccupied spot, they can have privacy in terms of other kids eavesdropping while still being out in the open, meaning that they won't get yelled at by a teacher for "going out of sight."

"Out of sight," on Rivendell's playground, means either *waaaay* down at the far end of the grassy field kids play soccer on, or in the section of the playground reserved for the preschoolers. The preschoolers' area is off-limits to the older kids, and one reason is because of the various plastic playhouses scattered about. Preschoolers play in the playhouses, whereas older kids have been known to sneak over and hide inside them or behind them.

Milla has heard rumors about things that happened out of sight. One is that several years ago, when Milla was too young to even know the fifth graders, a boy ducked into a bushy area, climbed over the fence, and just . . . left. He just walked away from the school and didn't come back. Why? He didn't like school, some kids said. Others claimed he hit a teacher *and* said the f-word earlier that day. He knew he was going to be suspended or even expelled, so why stick around?

Milla doesn't know if that rumor is true. But she knows from experience that strange things can happen out of sight. At the beginning of the year, Milla had a crying spell in the preschoolers' area, in a pink plastic house with white plastic shutters on the window. Shutters that could be closed, turning the house into a jail.

Modessa was with Milla, and she pretended to comfort Milla, but later Milla figured out that Modessa wanted her to cry and no doubt enjoyed seeing her cry.

You're with Max, she reminds herself. She wraps her arms around her ribs as she walks beside him. *Just stop, okay?*

But her conscience doesn't let her off the hook. *You need to help Elena*, it tells her.

Fine. I will. Now GO AWAY, she responds. She twitches without meaning to. She's like a horse twitching off a pesky fly. She hopes Max didn't notice.

"What do you want to talk about?" Max asks when they reach a vacant stretch of fence.

The wind continues to blow, but she no longer feels bold. She feels depressed because of the Elena thing. She also feels timid now that she and Max are alone. She's back to being a coward, basically.

She peeks at Max, who's gazing at her curiously. He has nice eyes. Non-evil eyes. It isn't his fault she's all tangled up inside.

"Um . . . how's your iPhone?" she asks, for lack of anything better to say. Max's parents bought him a phone as a replacement for Stewy, his hamster, although an iPhone *isn't* a hamster, of course. Even if it was, Stewy was Stewy, and Stewy is gone. Worse, Stewy is gone because of her. Last month, she stepped on Stewy, and it was an accident, but Stewy died anyway. And the worst part? Which is also the best part? Max forgave her. He knew she didn't mean to do it, and he forgave her, which is possibly the kindest thing anyone has ever done for her.

A hot sting of tears takes her off guard, but she blinks them back. She is here with Max, and Max is kind, and she will not cry.

"My iPhone?" Max says. "It's awesome. Do you want to see it sometime? I'd bring it to school, but cell phones aren't allowed."

Milla nods and takes a steadying breath. "I *do* want to see it. I would love to see it. But, um, both my moms have iPhones, so I've kind of seen them before."

"Oh," Max says.

"I bet you've got better apps than they do, though."

Max grins. "I bet I do, too. Do they have X-Plane?"

"I don't think so," Milla says. She has no idea what X-Plane is.

"Do they have More Toast?"

She shakes her head again. "What's More Toast?"

"An app that lets you make toast. It's so cool. You can put on pretty much any topping you can think of—butter, jam, sardines. Bacon. Fried chicken."

Milla wrinkles her nose. "Fried chicken? On toast?"

"And you can burn it if you want. Or not. You take bites by touching it, and it's got awesome crunching sounds."

"Cool," Milla says, although she can't wrap her head around what makes it so cool, actually.

"You can also get More Pizza, More Cookies, and More Cupcakes. Those are other apps," he explains.

"More Cupcakes?"

"That one's kind of for girls," he says. "You get to pick out the frosting and add sprinkles or chocolate chips or whatever."

Now *that* sounds fun. It helps Milla understand the

appeal of More Toast. "Can you put fried chicken on as a topping?"

Max laughs. "That would *rock.*"

"Can you burn them? I hope not. That would be so mean to those poor innocent cupcakes!"

"I don't have More Cupcakes, just More Toast," Max admits. "But if I did, I'd burn them. Burning the toast is fun, because it turns black and smoke comes out."

"You're so weird."

He shrugs. "Weird is more fun. Hey, I know—I'll download More Cupcakes and we can burn them together."

He leans against the fence. Milla leans against the fence. Her shoulders are *this close* to his, and Milla's breath catches. Modessa, Quin, and Elena are a distant memory, at least for now.

She wonders what would happen if she leaned just the teeniest bit to the left, so that her shoulders actually touched Max's shoulders. But she doesn't. She's not sure she's ready for that.

But then Max smiles his sweet Max-smile, and somehow their shoulders are touching. His skin is warm through his T-shirt, which is black with white letters. DECLARE VARIABLES, NOT WAR, it says. She doesn't understand what it means, but when has she ever understood what any of his shirts means?

His shirt doesn't matter. He does.

❋ Seven ❋

Katie-Rose and Violet have PE together after lunch. Violet isn't in a chatty mood, so Katie-Rose picks up the slack and chats enough for both of them. Yes, she's just that awesome.

"So, can I tell you something disturbing?" she asks as they walk into the gym. Sometimes they have PE inside; sometimes they have it outside. It depends on what Coach Wolff wants to do.

"And I'm serious when I say *disturbing*. I'm not just being dramatic."

"*You*, dramatic?" Violet says.

"Ha ha," Katie-Rose says. "The disturbing thing is that kids are saying they might play Spin the Bottle at Lock-In. Isn't that gross?"

"I guess," Violet says. "But *you* don't have to play."

"Hi, Katie-Rose!" Preston bellows, cupping his hands around mouth. "I'm right here, in case you wanted to throw something at me! Are you going to throw something at me?"

"In your dreams!" Katie-Rose calls back. Unless Coach Wolff has them play dodgeball, in which case, heck yeah she'll throw things at him.

Katie-Rose pulls Violet aside. "Spin the Bottle is a mushy game. We are too young to be mushy, Violet. Milla and Max are especially too young to be mushy. And what if Max has"—she lowers her voice, but ratchets up its intensity—"armpit studs?"

Violet does a double-take. "I'm sorry. *What*?"

Coach Wolff blows her whistle. Yes, she really does have a whistle, and boy, does she love blowing it. She blows her whistle and yells, "Students! Gather round!"

Violet meanders toward the milling students. Katie-Rose trots beside her. "Armpit studs. *Puberty.* All that stuff."

"Gross, Katie-Rose."

"I *know*," Katie-Rose says. "But . . ."

She bites her lip, because she hates puberty and is fascinated by puberty in equal measure. No, rewind. She just plain hates it (even if she *is* fascinated by it). She hates it because it MESSES THINGS UP.

Take, for example, the conversation she had with Milla yesterday. She called Milla after school to make sure Milla had signed up for trapeze lessons, and what did Milla do? She giggled. *Nervously.*

"Whoa, whoa, whoa," Katie-Rose said, knowing that nervous giggle far too well. "Are you telling me you *didn't* sign up for trapeze lessons?"

From the other end of the line came another nervous giggle. Whenever Milla feared Katie-Rose's wrath, out that nervous giggle popped.

"Milla! For the love of Cheese Puffs, *why?!*"

"Oh, Katie-Rose," Milla said.

"Don't you 'Oh, Katie-Rose' me," Katie-Rose said. "You have to sign up! Violet's going to, and Yasaman, and so it'll be all four of us. It'll be awesome!"

"Yaz signed up for trapeze lessons?" Milla asked.

Katie-Rose opened her mouth, then shut it. She decided to skip over that question, since she hadn't quite gotten around to telling Yasaman the happy news about how Katie-Rose filled out the sign-up sheet for her. "It's going to be awesome," she said instead. "Get a form tomorrow and turn it in, promise?"

"Katie-Rose . . ." Milla said, and despite being separated by entire streets and neighborhoods, Katie-Rose could envision Milla's expression perfectly. She'd be scrunching her face into a cute-but-apologetic grimace, the ever-ready counterpart to her nervous giggle. "Um, we're kind of too old for trapeze lessons, aren't we?"

"No!" Katie-Rose retorted. "That is the stupidest thing I've ever heard. That is *so* not an acceptable answer." Arguments flew out rapid-fire. "Why would we be too old? Are we too old for swinging? No. Are we too old for gymnastics? No. And trapeze lessons are, like, a mix of both of those things. Plus, if fifth graders were too old to take trapeze lessons, why would Josie come to Rivendell and say, 'Hey, all you cool fifth graders! Want to take trapeze lessons?'"

"Katie-Rose—"

"She wouldn't, that's why. And what about circus performers, huh? They're not kids. They're grown-ups, which means they're way older than we are. Are you saying circus performers are too old to be trapeze artists?"

There was silence on Milla's end of the line. Katie-Rose suddenly felt very loud, even though she was no longer speaking. She also had second thoughts about her use of the word *stupid*. Telling Milla that her reason for not signing up was the stupidest thing she'd ever heard might not have been the best—or nicest—strategy for persuading her friend to change her mind.

"Milla?" she said.

Milla, when she replied, didn't sound angry, which was good. She did sound sure of herself, however, and even a little tender, as though she didn't want to burst Katie-Rose's bubble. Which was bad.

"It's just, I don't want to be in the circus," Milla said.

After that, Katie-Rose got off quick, her cheeks burning. Instead of calling Yaz, as she'd planned, she went to her room and pulled out her dog-eared copy of *Your Growing Body*. It lives under her bed, and every so often she rereads certain sections, hoping to magically understand the business of growing up. Her FFFs seem to grasp the rules instinctively, which leaves Katie-Rose feeling... well ... stupid.

It also makes her feel naked. Not literally, as if she is prancing down the street completely nude, waving her arms over her head and singing, "La la la!" More like when someone's bathing suit bottom rides up and everyone can see her tan line. Brown skin below, codfish skin above. Or like a flipped-over roly-poly, waving its spindly legs frantically, yet failing to right itself and scurry off to catch its buddies. *That* kind of naked.

Katie-Rose brushes a stray hair out of her eyes. She wants to explain her fears to Violet, but she senses she lost her at "armpit studs." To tell the truth, she *might* have made up that term, but if she did, it was an accident.

She did not make up the term "breast buds," though. According to *Your Growing Body*, she herself will sprout "breast buds" one day, a prospect she finds unlikely. Last night she pulled her PJ top away from her body and peered through the neck hole. Not a bud was blooming.

Katie-Rose tugs on Violet's sleeve, and Violet glances down at her. For the record? Violet is tall and stunning and sports an impressive set of breast buds.

"I just think we need to be careful about not growing up too fast," Katie-Rose says. "Don't you?"

"Katie-Rose, please," Violet says, sounding weary.

Coach Wolff blows her whistle again, long and hard. "So here's what we're going to do!" she yells. "Form a circle! Are you forming a circle?!"

"I don't mean it in a *bad* way," Katie-Rose whispers, though she does. "We only get to be kids once, and we shouldn't waste it. So do you think I should tell Ms. Westerfeld about the Spin the Bottle rumor?"

"No, because what if other kids do want to play?" Violet says.

"But they shouldn't be allowed!"

"Yeah, only I'm not sure it's your decision, just like it wasn't your decision to sign me up for trapeze lessons." She frowns. "You thought I'd want to take *trapeze* lessons? Starting the week my *mom* came home?"

Katie-Rose's heart sinks. "So, um . . . you don't?"

"Uh, *no*. I called the girl who's teaching the class—"

"Her name's Josie."

"And asked her to take me off the list. But seriously, Katie-Rose. You can't control everything." She sighs. "Now hush, or Coach Wolff's going to yell at us."

Katie-Rose drops her gaze. She feels stupid *again*, just like she did after getting off the phone with Milla. She also thinks Violet is hardly one to talk. Maybe Katie-Rose does have control issues, but Violet does, too, especially when it comes to her mom. Like when she told Katie-Rose, Milla, and Yaz they couldn't come over yesterday even though they were two seconds from her house. What was that about? Does Violet plan on protecting her mom from the outside world forever?

Katie-Rose is immediately ashamed of herself. She knows her problems are nothing compared to Violet's.

Still. Why would Violet need to protect her mom from her *friends*?

"Katie-Rose!" Coach Wolff blares, making her flinch. "Are you aiding in the circle formation?"

"No, she's aiding in the malformed amoeba formation," Preston answers. In case anyone missed the put-down, he adds, "And *she's* the malformed amoeba."

Blah blah blah, sooooo clever, Katie-Rose thinks. She would throw another plum at Preston's big fat head if she could, and that's another reason not to grow up, since grown-ups aren't supposed to be plum throwers. Whatever.

"Be part of the solution! Not the problem!" Coach Wolff hollers. She blasts her whistle, and Katie-Rose wants to plug her ears. Instead, she takes a step forward and joins the dumb circle. She does a quick survey of her classmates and scowls. Almost everyone, it seems, is further along than she is.

Becca's parents have let her try champagne, which she says is delicious. Chance claims to have seventeen girlfriends, all in different states. Medusa—ugh,

Modessa—wears actual lipstick and could easily pass for a seventh grader, despite her ridiculous attire. She's paired a pink corduroy mini skirt with a white T-shirt pulled tight and knotted at the back. The shirt reads Evil Chick #1 . . . and guess who's wearing a shirt that says Evil Chick #3?

Yep, that would be Elena. Good ol' Elena, only *not* good anymore. Katie-Rose's jaw falls open as she takes a closer look. For the love of pickles, is *Elena* wearing lipstick, too?

A thought niggles in Katie-Rose's brain. It's slippery, and she can't quite catch hold of it, especially since Coach Wolff is still issuing team bonding commandments. But it has to do with Elena, and the lipstick, and the fact that up until this week, Katie-Rose, Yasaman, and Elena were the only fifth graders who didn't wear bras. Even Natalia wears a bra, whereas Katie-Rose neither owns a bra nor *wants* to own one. She doesn't even *want* to want one.

Can the same be said for Elena? *Or are those bra straps beneath her ridiculous shirt?* Elena is deliberately *not* looking at Katie-Rose, which is fortunate. If she was, she'd think Katie-Rose was a pervert for sure.

But Katie-Rose has seen the horror, and it is pink. Pink! The barest hint of two pink bra straps beneath Elena's white shirt, and Katie-Rose is so disgusted she shifts her gaze. Is that all it is, then? Is Elena, unlike Katie-Rose, foolish enough to want the pass-for-a-seventh-grader sophistication Modessa dangles before her like candy?

Katie-Rose would choose actual candy any day. Reese's Pieces always hit the spot. She's also, of late, developed a taste for Bit-O-Honeys. They're not chocolate, but they're chewy and long-lasting and lodge themselves deep in the cracks of her teeth, providing tongue-prodding entertainment for an entire class if Katie-Rose plays it right.

"So I take it everyone understands, then!" Coach Wolff bellows. "The bonding game I've chosen will bring you closer to your classmates, and why is that important? Because bonding turns individuals into a team! Got it?"

Violet rubs the spot between her eyebrows with one finger. Becca halfway raises her hand, then lowers it, probably remembering that Coach Wolff doesn't like questions, is terrible at answers, and occasionally spits on you if she addresses you directly.

"Are we allowed to trade one team member for another?" Preston asks Coach Wolff, his eyes trained on Katie-Rose. "If we're stuck with a dud?"

"No!" Coach Wolff yells. "A! In this class, you are a single unified team! B! There is no 'I' in teamwork! And C! In the Game of Life, you get what you get and you don't throw a fit! Do we understand each other?!"

Preston snaps his heels together and salutes, which would have been funny if Katie-Rose had thought to do it. "Yes, ma'am!"

"Then let's begin! Everyone will have a turn to ask the group a question! If the answer is yes, step forward! As your team leader, I will go first!"

Katie-Rose groans, along with most of the class.

"If you plan to attend this Friday's Lock-In, step forward!" Coach Wolff belts out.

Thomas steps forward, as do Katie-Rose and Violet. Brannen, Becca, and Natalia join them. Preston, Modessa, and Elena don't. But Elena clasps her hands behind her, reminding Katie-Rose of the way little kids sit on their hands when they know they're supposed to turn their listening ears on and not ask to be called on, even if they have something extremely important to say and really, *really* want to share it.

"Losers," Modessa sings quietly. Elena's lips wobble spazzily, resulting in an unconvincing smile.

Hmm, Katie-Rose wonders. Does the real Elena want to go to the Lock-In? Katie-Rose would bet dollars to doughnuts that she does. She just can't admit it and still hold on to the position of evil chick number three.

Oh, well. What's too bad for Elena is excellent for Katie-Rose. Rivendell has hosted Lock-Ins before, but Katie-Rose has never gone for fear that the cool kids *would* be there. What if no one hung out with her, and she spent the whole night alone while the other kids ran wildly through the school? Or what if her pj's were wrong? Because if you go to the Lock-In, you're supposed to show up in your pj's, a prospect Katie-Rose finds scary *and* exciting…kind of like puberty, come to think of it.

With the cool kids absent, Katie-Rose's puberty concerns won't come into play. She won't be judged in terms of bras or breast buds or the fact that she doesn't have a single boyfriend to Chance's seventeen across-the-nation girlfriends. And maybe the spin-the-bottle rumor is just that. A rumor. Plus, this is the first Lock-In Rivendell has hosted since Katie-Rose found her tribe of flower friends, and even if her FFFs are being poo-heads about taking trapeze lessons, there's never been a shred of doubt that they'd attend the Lock-In. All four girls are super excited about it, all four have officially signed up, and all four will have a BLAST.

So *ha ha* to Modessa and lipstick-wearing Elena and annoying Preston. Their loss is her gain. Now she can feel even *more* confident about going, which is a much better fit for her self-image, anyway.

"Excellent!" Coach Wolff says to the kids who stepped forward. "So much in common! Now step back into your original positions, and Becca, it's your turn ask a question!"

Becca looks like she'd rather pet a taxidermied possum. She swallows and says, "Um . . . if you like chocolate, step forward?"

This time everyone steps forward except Preston, Natalia, and Coach Wolff. Coach Wolff probably doesn't like chocolate because it's not made out of wheat germ and exclamation points. As for Preston, if he truly doesn't like chocolate, then that's just one more mark on his freak-o-meter. But Natalia? *Please.*

"Natalia, you do so like chocolate," Katie-Rose says.

"Nope," Natalia says. "Chocolate ith fattening, and I don't like foodth that are fattening. When I want thome-thing to munch on, I prefer carrotth."

Katie-Rose puts her hand on her hip. Just last month, Natalia made the absurd claim that she'd never had a soft drink in her entire life, but then guess what? Katie-Rose caught Natalia drinking a Coke AND eating green apple sour loops during lunch one day, in front of God and Katie-Rose and everyone.

"Does your ban on fattening foods apply to every-thing?" Katie-Rose says. "Even ... oh, let me think ... green apple sour loops?"

Natalia freezes. Her face has *possum-about-to-be-taxidermied* written all over it.

"'Cause last time I checked, green apple sour loops weren't on the food pyramid," Katie-Rose goes on. "I know they have the word *apple* in them, but I'm pretty sure they're not really a fruit."

Someone laughs. It sounds like Preston, of all people. But before Katie-Rose can verify the laugher's identity, Coach Wolff claps twice, indicating that everyone better shut their pie holes or else.

"Teachable moment!" she booms. She turns to Katie-Rose. "Katie-Rose! Who taught you about the food pyramid?!"

What a strange question. Who *did* teach her about the food pyramid? It seems like one of those nuggets of information she's always known and was most likely born with. "Um...my parents?"

Coach Wolff snorts. "As I suspected! Well, times have changed, kids, and now it's *your* turn to teach *them* about the food pyramid!" She scans the room. "That's your after-school assignment, got it?! When you go home today, I want each and every one of you to tell your parents that the food pyramid is gone!"

"Oh no!" Preston whispers. He somehow snuck up behind Katie-Rose without her noticing. "Someone stole the food pyramid!"

Katie-Rose's lips twitch, but she doesn't smile. Smiling at Preston's comments, even if they're funny, isn't an option.

"It's *gone*?" Becca asks. "Where did it go?"

Coach Wolff seems flummoxed by Becca's question. "*What?!* Nowhere! It simply turned into my plate!"

Now everyone is flummoxed.

"Huh?" Chance says.

"Why does it get to be *her* plate?" Preston whispers. She can feel his breath on her ear. "That's a little selfish, isn't it?"

Katie-Rose clamps her lips together. She will not smile, she will not smile, *she will not smile.*

Coach Wolff gives Preston the beady eyes. She strides over and barks, "Not *my* plate! *MyPlate!*"

Everyone gazes at her dumbly.

"Capital 'M' *My*!" she says. "Capital 'P' *Plate*! *MyPlate*, got it?!"

Everyone gazes at each other dumbly.

"'Say good-bye to the food pyramid, and say hello to MyPlate!'???" Coach Wolff says, as if this is a quote they all should know. She throws up her hands. "Do *none* of you read the annual report issued by the USDA?!"

There are a lot of consonants in Coach Wolff's question. One of them sends a spit droplet flying through the air, and *it hits Katie-Rose's cheek.* She recoils, Preston snickers, and Katie-Rose glares at him. That spit droplet should have gone to him. That spit droplet was his.

"I've heard of MyPlate," Natalia says goody-goody-ishly.

"Oh, bull-pooty," Katie-Rose mutters.

"And chocolate ithn't on it. That'th one reathon I don't like it. The other ith that it maketh me faint."

"Natalia, it does not," Katie-Rose says.

"Oh yeth, it duhth." Natalia stands taller. The metallic bits and bobs of her headgear gleam. "It wath at my cousin'th bar mitthvah." Her eyes take on a faraway look. "I fainted dead away."

"For real?" Becca asks. "You honestly and truly fainted?"

Katie-Rose doesn't know whether to believe Natalia or no. Either way, she's jealous. She's always wanted to faint.

Natalia puts her hand to her heart. "My poor parenth . . . Can you imagine? I *am* an only child, you know."

Coach Wolff blows her whistle. "Moving on! Modessa! Your turn to ask a question!"

"Hmm," Modessa says, touching her index finger to her berry-colored lips. Elena's lips are the exact same shade. *So* vile. "Step forward if you think you're normal."

She saunters forward. When Elena doesn't immediately join her, Modessa shoots her a look, and Elena jumps like she's been stung by a wasp. She practically falls over herself in her rush to obey her master. Natalia steps forward, too. So do Becca, Ava, Brannen, and—now, *this* is unexpected—Cyril.

Katie-Rose assumed that Cyril *liked* being not normal. That he understood what so few fifth graders do: That "normal" is b-o-r-ing *boring*.

Violet does not step forward, and Katie-Rose gives her a high five. Katie-Rose also stays put. *So there, Medusa*, is the message she sends silently through the air.

Modessa's head swivels toward Katie-Rose, and Katie-Rose's heart skips a beat. Did she speak the words out loud without realizing it?

Modessa's gaze flicks to Violet, but briefly, because Violet is blessed with a miraculous mental Saran Wrap that she can drop over her features at will. Meaning, Violet appears unfazed by Modessa regardless of the situation and regardless of what her real feelings might be. Katie-Rose would give anything to possess that skill, but she doesn't. Meaning, Katie-Rose is a far easier target. Katie-Rose knows it, and Modessa knows it. She's been toying with Katie-Rose for years now, after all.

And so she focuses her attention once more on Katie-Rose. She cocks her head and studies her, slowly, deliberately, and cunningly. Katie-Rose pleads with herself not to blush—*don't, don't,* please *don't*—but her body betrays her, and she feels the blood rush to her face.

Modessa smirks. She nudges Elena, and the two of them laugh. Elena's laugh starts off timidly, but grows stronger as other kids follow Modessa's lead. They're laughing at Katie-Rose, because yes, she's just that pathetic.

"Personally, I think they're full of it," Preston says into Katie-Rose's ear, and she's so startled, she squeals.

He laughs. "*You,* though. You *know* you're not normal, and I gotta say, I admire that in a girl."

Oh, he is so awful! But at least his insult snaps Katie-Rose out of her fog. She turns around, shoves him, and says, "You creeper! You shouldn't sneak up on people. Don't you know anything?"

Coach Wolff blows her whistle. She points at

Katie-Rose and yells, "You! No shoving!" She points at Preston and says, "And as for *you*, young man!"

Katie-Rose waits, eager to gloat when he gets in trouble.

But Coach Wolff doesn't seem to know what to reprimand Preston for. Finally she says, "*You* need to be more of a gentleman, young man!"

Preston laughs harder, and Katie-Rose thinks Coach Wolff should use *that* as his crime. Laughing at a teacher is surely punishable by death.

Except Preston makes it seem like he isn't laughing *at* Coach Wolff, or even at Katie-Rose. His laughter is round and happy and contagious, and the kids who were already laughing keep laughing, while the kids who weren't laughing join in. Violet holds her ground for a good two seconds, and then she bursts into laughter, too. She apologizes with her eyes, but Katie-Rose finds she can't even be mad. It's so good to see Violet laugh that the reason why doesn't matter.

A space opens between Katie-Rose's ribs, and a bubbly lightness rises within her. *Oh no.* She balls her hands

145

into fists, because she knows this feeling. Normally she would welcome it, but not now and not here. There is *no way* she's giving Preston that satisfaction!

"Yes, Preston, I *do* know that I'm not normal," she says. Her back is to the rest of the class, but she can feel them watching. She presses on. "I will *never* be normal, thank you very much, because I do not care to be normal."

"She doesn't *care* to be normal," Modessa repeats. "Did you hear that, Elena? As if she has any choice in the matter."

Briefly, Katie-Rose closes her eyes. She knows, in the grand scheme of things, that Modessa matters less than a fruit fly. Even so, she's scared of her. She probably always will be. But when push comes to shove, Katie-Rose *will* shove, regardless of how light-headed it makes her.

She turns back around. "Actually, *Medusa*, I have all the choice in the matter. I choose to be original, just like you choose to be an 'evil chick' who likes to put people down. And for the record? You think you're *so* hot, but you're not."

"Katie-Rose!" Coach Wolff barks. "Young ladies should *not* use the word *hot*! Young ladies should only say they're hot if their body temperature is elevated due to exertion or conditions of the climate! And in such conditions it is far more proper to say you are toasty! Or overheated!"

By now, almost everyone is laughing except for Katie-Rose and Coach Wolff. Oh, and Modessa, who glares at Katie-Rose as if she's trying to scorch her with rays of evilness.

"You said 'hot,'" Preston whispers in a singsong voice.

She whips around *again*. All this back-and-forth-ness is making her seriously dizzy.

"Listen, Preston," she says. "You just shut up."

Preston grins, and it's such a great, big grin—such a delighted grin—that despite herself, she almost grins back.

And then his words sink in. She replays her attack on Modessa, and she sways, because she *did* say "hot"! She feels like she might faint, which on the one hand would be awesome because she'd join the fainting club, but on the other hand would be awful, because when she came to, she'd be temporarily confused. She'd say, "Auntie Em? Auntie Em?" and for a moment she'd think she was a happy farm girl with a dog and a rainbow and an amazing singing voice. Then, when Preston threw cold water on her face, it would be all the worse, because she *wouldn't* be in Kansas. She'd still be in stupid California, and she'd still be the stupid girl who said "hot" during PE. She CANNOT believe she said the word "hot" in front of the whole class!

Later, she'll find eight crescent-shaped wounds in her palms from digging her fingernails so tightly into her flesh. Later still—during lunch with her besties—she'll inhale sharply and a half-chewed Oreo will lodge itself in her throat, sucked in when Katie-Rose is hit with a realization so shocking it makes her gasp. She'll have a coughing fit, and Violet will pound her on the back, and a cloud of Oreo crumbs will fly from her mouth and land in places unknown, never to be seen again.

Her realization, however, will remain.

During Coach Wolff's silly bonding game, Modessa said, "If you think you're normal, step forward." Everyone started off in a circle, and then Modessa asked her question, and then she and most everyone else proceeded to do exactly that: They stepped forward.

But while the majority of the class basked in the fake rays of their fake coolness, Preston stayed put in order to make his little joke about Katie-Rose—the joke about how she, at least, *knew* she wasn't normal. He whispered it into her ear just as he'd whispered his other dumb comments into her ear.

Only at the beginning of PE, Preston wasn't in whispering range of Katie-Rose. Of course he wasn't, because why on God's green earth would Katie-Rose plant herself next to *him*? Yet somehow during the course of the hour, he weaseled himself over to her, and there he stayed for the rest of class.

The fact that an annoying boy snuck behind her might not faze any *normal* girl, since boys are, by definition, annoying. So why did this realization nearly make Katie-Rose choke to death? Because it dawned on her that unless Preston possesses remarkably stretchy lips (unlikely) or a ghostly double that allows him to be in two places at once (even more unlikely), the rules of physics leave zero room for interpretation.

Preston was behind Katie-Rose when Modessa asked

her question. Preston *remained* behind her when Modessa and the other "normals" stepped forward. Otherwise, he wouldn't have been able to whisper dumb comments into her ear.

Therefore, only one conclusion could be drawn: Preston, like Katie-Rose and Violet, chose *not* to identify himself as a bland blob of Cream of Wheat. Preston, unlike Cyril and Modessa and the other kids in their PE class, *did* understand what so few fifth graders do: That "normal" is b-o-r-ing boring.

Or, infinitely more likely, he just wanted to mess with Katie-Rose's head.

Eight

Yasaman

At the end of the school day, Yaz finds Milla and drags her to Ms. Perez's room.

"We have to gather information about her so we can set her up with Mr. Emerson," Yaz tells her.

"We do?" Milla says.

"And you're better at girl stuff than I am. You know you are. And out of all of us, you're the only one who has any experience with, you know, *romance.*"

Milla bites her lower lip.

"Milla, I mean that in a good way!" Yaz says. She stops

in the hall and puts her hands on Milla's shoulders. "Max is really nice, and you are, too. And you make each other happy, right?"

Milla hesitates. "Um . . . I guess?"

Yaz leans closer and presses her forehead against Milla's. Now Milla has one huge eye instead of two regular size eyes. Yaz assumes she does, too, and that eventually the googliness of it will make Milla giggle, or at least smile.

"*Mill*-a," she says, stretching it out. "You. Are. Allowed. To be. *Happy*. Okay?"

Milla stares at Yaz with her big, blue, and slightly wobbly eye. She has yet to smile *or* giggle.

"Are you still thinking about . . . you know?" Yasaman says, referring to Modessa, Quin, and Elena. She doesn't want to say their names out loud, because as far as Yaz can tell, talking about them is what made Milla sad to start with.

It was during lunch. When the FFFs first sat down to eat, Milla was downright giddy. She'd spent all of morning break with Max, and her words bubbled out of her as she shared the details with Yaz and Violet and Katie-Rose.

"Yeah, yeah, yeah," Katie-Rose interrupted. "Only I think what happened to me is more important, so will you hush and let me tell it?"

It wasn't the nicest way to change the subject, but that's Katie-Rose. And when she told the story of Coach Wolff and the circle game, it *did* sober everyone up ... until Katie-Rose got to the part where she called Modessa out for being a big jerk, that is.

"*That'll* teach Modessa not to get all up in my grill," Katie-Rose huffed, and Yasaman giggled. She tried to turn the giggle into a cough, but it didn't fool anyone, and Katie-Rose got even huffier.

"Why do you find this funny?" she demanded. "This isn't funny. She got all up in my grill because I refuse to be a clone, and I could have *died*, and you're *laughing*?!"

"Sorry, sorry," Yasaman said. "It's just"—she paused, thinking back to something she'd heard her cousin Hulya say and wanting to get it right—"I didn't know you were so *gangsta*, yo!"

Katie-Rose did a spit take, making chocolate milk spurt from her nose. Violet grinned and shook her head. But Milla lowered her gaze and grew still. She was quiet throughout the rest of lunch.

In the hall outside Ms. Perez's room, Yasaman pulls back from Milla, just slightly. She lets go of Milla's shoulders and slides her fingers down until she reaches Milla's hands, which she takes. In her head, she tries out various questions: *Is it because Modessa used to be your friend? Are you mad at Elena for craving her approval? You don't want to be an "evil chick"... do you?*

She doesn't have to ask that last one. She knows Milla better than that. But since she can't decide what she *should* ask, she asks nothing, and instead says, "Well, if you are thinking about ... *you know* ... Elena ..."

Color rises in Milla's cheeks.

Yaz hurries to fill the silence. "You don't have to, is all. I mean, you can if you *want* to, but you don't have to worry about anyone's problems except your own." She frowns. "Well, and mine. Or not *mine*, but ours, and by that I mean all of us—you, me, Katie-Rose, and Violet. Because friends take care of friends. And that goes for family, too, and I guess nice people in general, and I suppose sometimes we worry about people we don't even know . . ."

Okay, she is making this overly complicated. She squeezes Milla's hands and ducks her head, coaxing Milla to look at her. "I'm not making much sense, am I?"

Milla meets her eyes. Two blue eyes, two brown eyes. No more big wobbly eyes. She gives a small laugh and says, "*Much* sense? Yaz, you're not making *any* sense. What happened to setting up Ms. Perez and Mr. Emerson?"

Relief makes Yasaman woozy. "Right. *Right*. That *is* what we're here to work on. I posted a Big Begonia about it this morning, but I'm guessing you haven't read it."

Milla shrugs. "We've been at school. I haven't been online."

"Um, right again." She lets go of Milla's hands and adjusts her *hijab*. "Well, a while back we decided that getting Mr. Emerson and Ms. Perez together was going to be our next flower power project. We were going to call it Project Teacherly Love."

"You mean Teacherly *Lurrrrve*," Milla says.

"Omigosh, you're right!" Yaz says. "You *do* remember!"

She darts forward and peeks inside Ms. Perez's room. "She's there, and she's by herself. Let's go!"

Milla stalls, digging in with her heels as Yaz pulls on her. "But what are we—"

"Yasaman?" Ms. Perez says, appearing in the doorway. "Oh, hi, Camilla. Do you girls need something? Come on in."

Milla gives Yaz a *you're in trouble* look. Yaz smiles sweetly, first at Milla and then at Ms. Perez.

"Well, um, we're doing a survey," she says as she follows Ms. Perez back into the room. She drags Milla with her.

"Oh?" Ms. Perez asks, perching on top of her desk.

"Yes, and we want to interview you, if that's okay," Yasaman says. She pulls up two chairs. She sits in one, and Milla takes the other. Then she hops up and grabs a piece of paper, a pencil, and a book to bear down on from the supply shelf. She drops back into her chair, only slightly out of breath. She positions the pencil over the piece of paper. "So can we?"

Ms. Perez smiles. "Sure. But what's this survey about? And what's it for?"

Yaz falters. "Well . . . um . . ."

"It's just for fun," Milla supplies. "We want to compare what people like and don't like and see what patterns emerge."

"Yeah," Yaz says, making a concentrated effort not to gape at her friend. *And see what patterns emerge?* Yaz is so impressed. Milla is making it sound so real!

"And we'll probably share the results with my mom," Milla adds. "She's a caterer. She's always interested in finding out more about her target demographic."

"Am I her target demographic?" Ms. Perez asks. She seems amused.

"Do you enjoy good food, or are you more of Burger King kind of person?" Milla asks.

"Both," Ms. Perez says, "though I avoid Burger King as much as I can." She glances at her thighs. "I don't always succeed."

"Then you're totally her demographic," Milla says with authority. "And you're right not to go to Burger King, because Burger King is super unhealthy. But if you're worried about, like, your weight, you shouldn't be. Women are meant to have curves, that's what my mom says."

For some reason, this makes Ms. Perez smile.

"That is a great mentality," Ms. Perez says, "and I think it's great that she's passing it along to you. My mother was always encouraging me to go on a diet. She still is, for that matter."

Milla clucks. "Everyone's different. Like, even though my Mom Joyce agrees that women are meant to have curves, she herself is more of a toothpick. But it's not because she's on a diet. She was just born that way. And my Mom Abigail is the exact opposite, right, Yaz?"

Yaz isn't entirely comfortable discussing the body types of adults. But she nods, because Mom Abigail does have the exact opposite body type of Mom Joyce. Mom Abigail is plump and rosy-cheeked and smells like vanilla. She wears soft T-shirts and flowy skirts, and she's almost always smiling. Yasaman can't imagine her looking any other way.

"But they're both equally beautiful," Milla says. "That's what I think, anyway."

Ms. Perez tilts her head, regarding Milla as if she's a rare butterfly that randomly flew into her room. "You know, Mr. Emerson once told me that he learns more from his students than they do from him," she says. "If they're all like you, Camilla, I bet he does."

Yasaman blinks twice. Ms. Perez just brought up Mr. Emerson *all by herself*, and Yaz should be excited. Instead, she is struck by an unwanted stab of jealousy. Ms. Perez is *her* teacher, not Milla's, and she—Yasaman—is Ms. Perez's favorite student. Not Milla.

She stares at her blank sheet of paper, feeling dumb. Then something nudges her knee. It's the toe of Ms. Perez's glossy red wedge pump.

"Not that I'm surprised, seeing as how you're one of Yasaman's best friends," she says, addressing Milla but looking at Yaz. "Yasaman's pretty special. She's taught me a few things as well."

Warmth spreads through Yasaman, melting her jealousy away. She and Ms. Perez share a smile.

"So, speaking of Mr. Emerson," Milla says. "Do you two spend time together outside of school?"

She asks this with complete innocence, thrilling Yasaman with her courage. It reminds her that Milla is pretty special, too—not that she ever truly forgot.

Ms. Perez opens her mouth, then closes it. She laughs. "Um ... is this part of the survey?"

Milla lifts her shoulders prettily. "Just curious. He's always saying what good taste you have, that's all."

Ms. Perez turns pink. "He is? He said that?"

"Not just once, but lots," Milla says, and even Yasaman thinks, *Wow. Really?* Then she realizes that Milla is probably telling a bit of a white lie for the sake of Project Teacherly Lurve. Meaning that Mr. Emerson might or might not have commented on Ms. Perez's good taste, but it surely can't hurt to toss the idea out there, especially since Ms. Perez *does* have good taste. Even if Mr. Emerson hasn't said so out loud to Milla, that doesn't mean he doesn't agree.

"Well, I'm sure it's just because I laugh at his jokes," Ms. Perez says.

"Sometimes he's funny," Milla says casually. "I like people who are funny. What about you, Yaz?"

Yaz snaps to attention. It's time she contributed to Project Teacherly Lurve instead of letting Milla carry all the weight. "Yes! Funny is good!" she says with too much enthusiasm. She takes it down a bit. "As long as it's *nice* funny. Right, Ms. Perez?"

"I—I suppose," Ms. Perez says.

"Cool. I'll write that down," Yasaman says.

Likes ppl who r nice-funny.

She grins at her teacher, who still seems flustered.

"What about baked goods?" Milla asks. "Do you like baked goods?"

Baked goods?! Yaz thinks. For some reason, the term strikes her as funny.

"As long as they're good baked goods," Ms. Perez replies, and Yasaman laughs out loud.

"Likes good baked goods," she says aloud, neatly printing the words on the next line.

"I thought you said this was a survey," Ms. Perez says.

"It is!" Milla insists. "What about music? What kind of music do you listen to?"

Ms. Perez eyes her. "How does that have to do with your mom's target demographic?"

"It just does. Everything does," Milla says. "So . . . ?"

Ms. Perez holds out her hands, as if waiting for the

answer to drop down into them. She says, "Well, I listen to all kinds of music."

"So does Mr. Emerson!" Milla exclaims. She quickly adds, "And so do I. I really do love all kinds of music. Write that down, Yaz."

Yaz does, ducking her head to hide her smile. She wants to hug Milla, that's how happy she is that Milla's going along with her plan. Also, Yaz was right: Milla is far better at romantic-ish stuff than Yaz is. No wonder she's the only one of the flower power girls to have a boyfriend.

Milla leans forward. "Moving on. Favorite animal?"

"To eat? Or to listen to music with?"

"What? Neither!" Milla says. And then, "*Ohhhh.* You were being funny! Ms. Perez is funny just like Mr. Emerson, Yaz. Did you know that?"

"I did," Yasaman says. "She's not as corny, though." She lifts her eyebrows as a question of her own comes to mind. "What about corn? Do you like corn?"

"Does she like *corn?*" Milla says, giggling.

"That's important for our survey!" Yaz protests. "It's just as important as what her favorite animal is!"

"Mr. Emerson calls us 'children of the corn' some-times," Milla says.

"He does?" Ms. Perez says.

"*There* you guys are," says Katie-Rose, barging into Ms. Perez's room. She flattens her back against the wall and pants, as if to suggest she's being chased. Yasaman highly doubts she is. "Milla, your mom's waiting for you in the pickup lane. And whose favorite animal? Mine is a cougar, or maybe a jaguar, because they're fast and they live in South America. And because they're cats, and I just plain like cats. Yup, I'm a cat person."

She pauses to breathe. She also waves at Ms. Perez. "Hi, Ms. Perez. Are you a cat person or a dog person?"

Ms. Perez takes the whirlwind that is Katie-Rose in stride, saying simply, "Hello, Katie-Rose. I like both cats and dogs."

"That is *so weird*," Milla says. She gets to her feet, the movement lifting strands of blond hair from her face. The strands sway as she shakes her head in amazement. "Mr. Emerson is a dog and a cat person, too! Write that down, Yaz. We'll go over the results later. Bye!"

Milla leaves the room as Yaz writes it down:

Cat-and-dog person.

"Strangest survey ever," Ms. Perez murmurs.

"Survey? I love surveys," Katie-Rose says, pushing off the wall and coming to stand by Yaz. "Ask me anything. Fire at will!"

"Definitely," Yaz tells her. She stands. "But later, 'kay? My mom's probably here by now, too."

"What if you were a boy, and your *name* was 'Will'?" Katie-Rose says.

"Huh?"

"What if your name was 'Will,' and there was a firing squad nearby, only you weren't the one being shot," Katie-Rose says, as if her train of thought is perfectly logical. "But then the commander-in-chief dude yelled, 'Fire at will!' Fire at *Will*. Get it?"

Ms. Perez groans and puts her hands over her face.

"Fire at Will," Katie-Rose repeats. "That would suck!"

Yasaman is embarrassed. Katie-Rose shouldn't say *suck*. "Why would there be a firing squad nearby?" she points out. "When is there ever a firing squad just randomly nearby, and why would—oh, never mind."

Ms. Perez laughs. "You girls are too much."

"Katie-Rose might be. I'm not," Yasaman says.

"You have a point," Ms. Perez replies, prompting Katie-Rose to say, "*Heyyy*!"

"Oh, Katie-Rose, I'm kidding," Ms. Perez says. She pauses. "Actually, I'm not. But you know I love your spunkiness." She pushes off her desk, her red wedge heels clacking against the floor. "And Yasaman, you might not be giving yourself enough credit. I think Katie-Rose's spunk is rubbing off on you, hmm?"

"It is?" Yaz says.

"The trapeze class," Ms. Perez says. "I can't tell you how pleased I am to see you stepping out of your comfort zone."

Yaz knits her eyebrows. She secretly does want to step out of her comfort zone, that's true. She wishes she could be bigger, better, *more*, just like she said in her Big Begonia post, just as she wishes she could go swooping through the sky, weightless as a feather.

But what in the world is Ms. Perez talking about? And why is Katie-Rose slinking in sneaky sideways steps toward the door? She freezes when Yasaman spots her. She plasters on a wide-eyed smile.

"Wh-what do you mean?" Yaz asks Ms. Perez.

Ms. Perez regards Yasaman fondly, as if Yaz is being silly, or modest. "I was surprised to see that you'd filled out an information slip, I admit it. But *so* proud, Yasaman."

Specks of light dance around the periphery of Yasaman's vision. She puts her hand on her desk to steady herself. It's possible, she supposes, that it was the mention of trapeze lessons that nudged her flying daydream to the surface. But she did not actually *sign up* for trapeze lessons. That is utterly *im*possible.

"Yaz?" Ms. Perez says. "Maybe you should sit back down, sweetie. You look like you're about to faint. And Katie-Rose, don't leave yet, just in case."

Yasaman turns back to Katie-Rose, who is now almost all the way to the door. *Yaz, we have to sign up,* she'd insisted when the forms were passed out. *Okay? Okay. Good!*

"Katie-Rose?" Yasaman says. Her mouth is dry. "Did you put my name on one of the sign-up sheets?"

Katie-Rose rocks back and forth. "Well, what you've got to under*stand*, you see, is . . . um . . ."

"Did you—" Her throat closes. She tries again. "Did you put down my parents' names? And my phone number?"

Ms. Perez's hand is on Yasaman's shoulder, guiding her back into her seat. "Yasaman, I'm going to get you some water. Stay put. Katie-Rose, stay with her."

Ms. Perez must make a disapproving thing out of her mouth as she hurries out of the room, or maybe with her eyes, because Katie-Rose shrinks back.

Now it's just the two of them. More memories float up, like the name of the girl teaching the class—*Josie*. And what she mentioned at the end of her speech about how she'd call the parents of everyone who signed up and tell them not to worry, she wouldn't let anyone die. *Once your parents give their permission, you're good to go,* she said. *Cool?*

Yasaman imagines Josie calling her house and asking to speak to her *baba*. She stares at her friend, who looks like a stranger, and whispers, "You did, didn't you?"

"Fine, I did. Yes!" Katie-Rose confesses. "But it was an accident! I *swear*."

Yasaman is light-headed. Everything's foggy.

"Anyway, we can fix it," Katie-Rose insists. She takes a step toward Yasaman, twisting her hands. "We'll call Josie—*I'll* call Josie—and tell her it was a

167

misunderstanding. A mistake. Will you *please* quit looking at me like that?"

Except Yasaman doesn't *know* how she's looking at Katie-Rose, which makes it hard to stop.

"I'm sorry, I'm sorry, I'm sorry!" Katie-Rose pleads. "It honestly was a mistake, and all I can say . . . all I can *say* is . . ." Her voice wobbles as she utters the words she really, really shouldn't. "Oopsy daisy?"

_____

Yaz, hi! I just this second read your post from this morning, and YES! I am game for Project Teacherly Lurve! I don't know what I can do, but I'll start thinking about it, k?

But, listen. About the butterfly bush. It sounds like you really love it, huh? I'm sure my mom would, too, but I was wondering . . . well, do you think maybe you could just keep it? Like, forever?

I totally don't want to sound rude or ungrateful, and anyway, I'm probably just being dumb. It's just that I don't want my mom to feel like she has to take care of anything but herself right now. And I'm not sure I'm up for taking care of anything else, either, even a plant. Cuz what if it died, you know?

You don't HAVE to, obviously. But if you *want* to, I would really really really appreciate it. I cld just, like, tell Milla that my dad is allergic, and that I didn't mention it earlier cuz I didn't want to hurt her feelings.

It's your call. Just let me know, k?

xxx,

Violet 😊

Wednesday, October 19

❉ Nine ❉

Katie-Rose

Once upon a time, a certain person—whose name is Max's mom, or, if the situation calls for formality, Mrs. Max's Mom—said something about Katie-Rose. She said it out loud and into the air, and although Katie-Rose's ear wasn't nearby at the time, Max's ear was, and Max's ear took in the comment and stored it in his brain. Later Max's mouth spat the comment out in front of Katie-Rose's ear, and it landed in *Katie-Rose's* brain, where it continues to live to this day.

The gist of the comment was this: that Katie-Rose

sometimes hides behind her beloved video camera, using it as a shield to protect her from facing the world head on.

Katie-Rose doesn't think Max's mom said it to be mean, and she doesn't think Max repeated it to Katie-Rose to be mean, either. Because neither Max nor his mom is a mean type of person.

Anyhoodle, there might be a kernel of truth to what Max's mom said, and that is why Katie-Rose brings her sunshine yellow Sony Cybershot to school on Wednesday. She brings it *on purpose*, with the specific intention of using it as a shield, and she tells herself that hiding behind her camera on purpose is different from hiding behind it accidentally.

This is an important distinction, because it means she's not in denial. She's just smart. She knows full well that Yasaman might still be upset with her, even though she did everything within her power to fix the trapeze lesson misunderstanding, just like she promised. She e-mailed Yaz last night and told her so, and then she called her, wanting to talk it out with voices rather than flat black computer words.

She didn't get to, though. Instead, she reached the

Tercans' answering machine, so she sang a special and impromptu song in the hopes of melting Yasaman's heart. She made up the lyrics on the spot, and she used the tune from a song her parents used to sing to her about how much they loved her.

Katie-Rose's version went like this:

I love you Yas-a-man,
Oh yes, I do-ooo,
I don't love anyone
Like I love you-oo-oo.
When you're not wi-ith me,
I'm blue-OOO-ooo!

(dramatic pause, and also a quick chance to catch her breath)

Oh Yas-a-man,
I (beat) *love* (beat) *you!*

Katie-Rose was proud of her song, and thought for sure that Yaz would call her back. She didn't. Then it got to be eight o'clock, and Katie-Rose knew she wouldn't, because of her dad's strict rules.

Hence the video camera this morning, a.k.a. her shield. If for some nutso reason Yaz *is* still mad, Katie-Rose might accidentally get teary, and NO WAY does she plan on parading her tears in front of the other fifth graders. She is to be known as tough Katie-Rose, not *wah-wah* babyish Katie-Rose.

During art, the right moment for approaching Yaz presents itself. Ten minutes into class, Ms. Viney steps out to take one of her many breaks, and since no teacher equals no chance of adult interference, Katie-Rose seizes the moment.

FADE IN:

INTERIOR RIVENDELL ELEMENTARY—MS. VINEY'S ART CLASS—MORNING

KATIE-ROSE (off-screen)

Hey, people! I am filming you guys, just so you know! I'm not going to make you sign releases. Don't worry. Just act normal and pretend I'm not here!

Quin glances up from a long table covered with brown paper. The class is working on a mural called Nature Is Beautiful, and Quin is drawing what looks like a giraffe-hippopotamus hybrid.

QUIN

Not a problem. Already was.

KATIE-ROSE (off-screen)

Oh, aren't you the comedian. Hardy hardy har. But guess what?

QUIN

What?

KATIE-ROSE (off-screen)

You're not ignoring me. You're looking straight at me.

Quin sticks out her tongue, then returns to her drawing. She adds a tail to her . . . giraffamus. She really isn't the best artist.

Katie-Rose swings her Cybershot around, getting

a panoramic shot of Ava, Melody, and Preston, who mugs for the camera by doing a cheesy point-and-wink combination.

PRESTON

Well he-e-e-y there, television audience, and yes, I am that good-looking, aren't I? Ah, sorry, no time for autographs. Ouch, I know. But we television stars don't interact with the riffraff. It's a matter of policy. I hope you—

Katie-Rose keeps the camera moving. Shelves and bins stocked with art supplies fill the revolving shot until finally the image grows still. Katie-Rose has found her subject.

KATIE-ROSE (off-screen)

(gulping)

Hi there, Yasaman. Hi there, old-buddy-old-pal.

Yasaman is drawing butterflies around a green bush with purple blossoms. She pauses and gives Katie-Rose a small smile, which *could* be read as a positive sign, except it's a things-are-fine-but-not-quite-right smile.

YASAMAN

Hi, Katie-Rose.

The image jiggles as Katie-Rose walks toward her. She could use the zoom function, but Katie-Rose isn't after a close-up. What Katie-Rose wants is privacy. Well, from behind the safety of the camera, that is.

KATIE-ROSE (off-screen)

That's a good drawing. Is it a butterfly bush?

Yasaman picks up an orange marker and colors in a butterfly's wings.

YASAMAN

Mmm-hmm.

KATIE-ROSE (off-screen)

Well, it's really pretty. And I'm sorry again about

. . . you know. Hey, did you hear my song last night? On your answering machine?

YASAMAN

I did. We all did. Nigar hit "play" over and over again, until my dad said, "*Durma*! I can't take it anymore!" and marched over and hit "delete."

She glances at Katie-Rose, and her lips twitch, a sign she *might* be thawing.

YASAMAN (CONT'D)

You're a strange person, you know.

KATIE-ROSE (off-screen)

I do know! I'm also a very *delightful* person, with a multitude of delightful personality traits.

She grips the camera more tightly.

KATIE-ROSE (off-screen) (CONT'D)

I'm, uh, also a very very *sorry* person, about . . .

um ... the thing I'm sorry about. Although I still don't understand why you don't want to.

Yasaman sighs.

YASAMAN

It's not that I don't *want* to. It's just complicated. My dad ...

KATIE-ROSE (off-screen)

What? Doesn't believe in trapeze lessons?

YASAMAN

It's not *that*—although I don't know, maybe he doesn't. But don't you remember what a big deal it was to get him to let me go to the Lock-In?

KATIE-ROSE (off-screen)

Yeah. So?

YASAMAN

So trapeze lessons would be even worse, in his

mind. Because of the boys, and doing stuff like
flipping upside down—

                    KATIE-ROSE (off-screen)
                        (interrupting)
He doesn't want anyone seeing your underwear?!

                         YASAMAN
No! It's not that. It's just complicated, like I said.

                    KATIE-ROSE (off-screen)
So he *does* want people seeing your underwear?

                         YASAMAN
                        (frustrated)
No!

                    KATIE-ROSE (off-screen)
                        (snortling)
I guess not, since he only agreed to the Lock-In
on the condition that you wouldn't wear paja-

mas. You're going to be the only kid not wearing pajamas, you know. That still makes me laugh.

YASAMAN

Great. Thanks.

KATIE-ROSE (off-screen)

Omigosh. Oh, Yasaman, I'm a total jerk, aren't I?

The image jiggles as Katie-Rose thwacks herself on the head.

KATIE-ROSE (off-screen) (CONT'D)

Seriously, sometimes even I don't know what's wrong with me. I am *so* sorry, Yaz. I'm sorry for being a jerk about the pj's, I'm sorry for bugging you about your dad, and most of all I'm sorry for the whole trapeze fiasco.

She holds out her arm, a bit of which shows up in the shot.

You can hit me if you want. Do you want to hit me?

YASAMAN

I don't want to hit you, Katie-Rose. And you don't have to keep apologizing. You talked to Josie and told her to take my name off the list, right? So stop worrying.

For a moment, Katie-Rose is overjoyed. Yasaman forgives her! She can stop worrying! Then her stomach does a twisty-turvy thing, because of something she'd rather not mention. Though Katie-Rose did call Josie last night, she didn't exactly *talk* to her, not in the way Yasaman probably thinks. As in, there was no conversation, per se. As in, only one person did the talking, and it was Katie-Rose, and it was after Josie's phone said, "Beep! Leave a message!"

YASAMAN (CONT'D)

Anyway, I was a complete spaz about it, so I'm sorry. I totally overreacted.

KATIE-ROSE (off-screen)

No, you didn't.

YASAMAN

Yes, I did.

KATIE-ROSE (off-screen)

No, no, no.

YASAMAN

Yes, yes, yes.

Yasaman giggles, and Katie-Rose allows herself to giggle back, even though there's kinda sorta something else Katie-Rose didn't mention when she e-mailed Yaz last night.

The something else she didn't mention isn't a big deal, though. Katie-Rose really doesn't think it is. It's just that in addition to reaching Josie's voicemail instead of the real Josie, the voicemail thingie might possibly have cut Katie-Rose off before she was done leaving her message. A weird staticky sound blared into Katie-Rose's ear soon after she started talking, and then the phone died and a dial tone came on. When Katie-Rose called back, a computer-generated voice said, "This mailbox is full. Please try again. This mailbox is full. Please try again."

But. For now, she can't try again. She can only try to appease sweet Yaz.

KATIE-ROSE (off-screen)

You weren't the spaz. I was. And if you keep arguing with me, then we will just have to agree to disagree.

Yasaman finally gives Katie-Rose a genuine smile.

YASAMAN

If you insist.

KATIE-ROSE (off-screen)

(beaming)

I do. So . . . we're good?

YASAMAN

Yeah, we're good. Hey, did you read the Big Begonia I posted to LuvYaBunches.com?

KATIE-ROSE (off-screen)

Um . . . yes! And it was awesome. Yay, butterflies!

YASAMAN

What about Project Teacherly Lurve? Are you up for it? Violet and Milla both are.

KATIE-ROSE (off-screen)

(hemming and hawing)

Well, I *would* be, but I'm just . . . I'm kind of not into romance at this particular juncture in my life. You know?

Yasaman pulls her eyebrows together.

YASAMAN

What particular juncture in your life? What

187

does that even mean? Anyway, don't you want you-know-who to make a love connection?

KATIE-ROSE (off-screen)

Listen. It's not you; it's me.

YASAMAN

That makes no sense, either! Katie-Rose, c'mon. This really means a lot to me.

KATIE-ROSE (off-screen)

I know, I know. I'm just not in a lovey-dovey space right now. You can understand that, right?

Preston's face suddenly fills the screen, and it is so surprising—and so huge—that Katie-Rose squeals.

PRESTON

Hello, ladies. You might want to evacuate the area, because I just let one rip.

KATIE-ROSE (off-screen)

Gross, Preston. Thanks for sharing.

PRESTON

(grinning)

Sharing means caring. Uh-oh, here comes another one.

A loud fart makes Yasaman recoil. She delicately sniffs the air and makes a horrible face.

YASAMAN

Ewww! Please stop, I beg of you!

PRESTON

Hey, all I can do is let nature take its course. That's the way I roll, lady.

He gestures at the mural, which is of random animals and banana trees and vines. The mural started off as plain old nature, but somehow morphed into Costa Rica or Brazil or some other jungle-y place.

PRESTON (CONT'D)

And remember: Nature Is Beautiful.

KATIE-ROSE (off-screen)

Gross, Preston.

Ava gags. Katie-Rose shifts the camera's focus to capture not only her reaction, but the reaction of everyone else in the class. Grossed out though she is, she knows this is great footage. Plus, she has two brothers. It's not as if this is new territory. In fact, she's actually not as grossed out as she pretends to be … not that she's planning on telling Preston that.

AVA

(turning green)

Oh my God, Preston. What did you have for breakfast?

PRESTON

Sausage, sausage, and more sausage. Mmmm.

He lifts his eyebrows.

PRESTON (CONT'D)

Uh-oh. Here comes another.

He shifts his focus, as if concentrating on something invisible and inward. A long, rippling bbbbbppppfffff sound is heard.

PRESTON (CONT'D)

Ahhhhh.

Brannen appears in the shot and gives Preston a high five.

BRANNEN

Nice one, dude.

AVA

I am seriously going to barf. I mean it, you guys!

KATIE-ROSE (off-screen)

Please don't. Or if you do, not on me.

PRESTON

Why? Are you afraid of barf?

KATIE-ROSE (off-screen)

(sarcastically)

Yes, Preston, I'm afraid of barf. I'm so afraid, I have nightmares about it.

Preston looks delighted.

PRESTON

Really? You have nightmares about barf?

KATIE-ROSE (off-screen)

Geez Louise. No, I just don't want it on my camera.

PRESTON

For her barf to reach your camera, she'd have to projectile vomit. Ava, can you make yourself projectile vomit?

AVA

Please stop talking about it. I mean it.

QUIN

Remember that time in second grade? When we had a substitute, and Chance threw up all over the place? And then Ava threw up, and then everybody in the whole class threw up?

KATIE-ROSE (off-screen)

I wasn't in that class. I had Mr. Chomsky for second grade.

PRESTON

I remember. It was awesome.

KATIE-ROSE (off-screen)

More like awesome sauce, you mean.

Preston laughs, and when he holds up his hand to her for a high five, she slaps her palm against his. She tells herself it would be rude not to.

Ava stumbles backward, finds the wall, and sinks down until she's sitting on the floor. She closes her eyes and moans.

QUIN

Somebody better get her a bucket.

KATIE-ROSE (off-screen)

Why don't you get her a bucket?

QUIN

Because I don't know where a bucket is.

Brannen raises his hand, despite the fact that Ms. Viney isn't there to call on him.

BRANNEN

Ooo! Ooo! I know where a bucket is. Mrs. Gundeck keeps one in her room just in case, because she is afraid of vomit. For real!

PRESTON

Dude, I know. That one day when you hacked up
that glob of spit—

BRANNEN

(interrupting)

It wasn't spit. It was a scab, from having my
tonsils taken out.

Ava moans more loudly. She rests her arms on her
knees and her forehead on her arms. Her long hair falls
in a curtain over her face.

AVA

(muffled)

Do not bring up that scab. If you bring up that
scab—

PRESTON

(interrupting gleefully)

And you said, "Hey, Ava! Look!" And Ava said—

AVA

(still muffled but more desperate)

I'm going to throw up. Not kidding.

BRANNEN

And Mrs. Gundeck ended class and sent us
outside. It rocked.

PRESTON

It did indeed. And all because Mrs. Gundeck is
afraid of barf, just like Katie-Rose.

Katie-Rose zooms in on Preston's face. Katie-Rose has Mrs.
Gundeck for German just like all the other fifth graders,
but she isn't in the same German class as Preston.

KATIE-ROSE (off-screen)

I am not afraid of barf, and I am nothing like
Mrs. Gundeck. Take it back.

PRESTON

No, thanks.

He turns sideways and slaps his butt.

PRESTON (CONT'D)

I'm about to let another one rip. Wanna get a
close-up?

The girls in the class protest and say "ewwwww." Ava
gags and hangs her head so low that her hair grazes
the floor.

YASAMAN

Turn off the camera, Katie-Rose. Stop encouraging him.

PRESTON

Yeah, stop encouraging me, Katie-Rose. Unless
you *want* to encourage me.

He squats, pulls in his fists, and waggles his fanny
suggestively. Yasaman covers her eyes, then separates
her fingers and peeks up at Katie-Rose. She makes a
funny expression that only Katie-Rose can see.

(mouthing the words dramatically)

Turn. Off. The. Camera!

Katie-Rose's heart lifts. This is the Yasaman she missed, and with things back to normal, she's happy to turn off the camera. Heck, she doesn't need it anymore. It's true that the trapeze issue still hangs over her head, but she tells herself that surely her message to Josie went through.

She'll try again this afternoon, just in case. Until then, there's nothing more she can do.

FADE TO BLACK

❈ Ten ❈

Violet

During morning break, Violet feigns a headache. "I think I'll go get some Advil from the office," she tells Yasaman and Katie-Rose.

"Do you want me to come with you?" Yasaman says. She rises from the bench they're sitting on. "I'll come with you."

Violet pushes her back down. "No, stay. I'll be back in, like, five seconds."

"They won't give you Advil without a note from a parent!" Katie-Rose calls to her back. "Just so you know!"

Milla spots her as she passes the tetherball stand and hurries to her side.

"Violet?" she says. "Are you okay?"

"Got a headache, no big deal," she says. She gestures at Max, who's waiting for Milla to return. They'd been leaning against the tetherball pole together. It was very cute. "Go back to your knight in shining armor."

"He's not my—" She makes a sound that's half indignant, half pleased. "Get real. I don't need a knight in shining armor."

"I know, but go back to Max-Max anyway. I'm fine."

In the office, she hesitates before approaching Mr. McGreevy, the young office assistant whose British accent charms all the parents and most of the students, too. She hesitates because she doesn't want an Advil. What she wants is to use the phone. Except she also *doesn't* want to use the phone. Frankly, she doesn't know what she wants, and it's making her antsy.

She got the butterfly bush issue cleared up, which is excellent. Yaz said she'd be thrilled to keep it and gave Violet the biggest hug ever, and Milla seemed totally fine with the regifting.

But the issue of her mom is *not* cleared up. In fact, it's *messed* up, that's what it is. Sometimes when she's with her mom, it's great. Other times, it's not. Sometimes Violet can't bear to be near her; other times, she can't bear to be apart. And when she's at school, well, that's the worst, because she has no control over the matter. It drives her crazy!

Ugh, wrong word. Forget that word. Plus, the truth of the matter is that she *does* need breaks from her mom. It's just, she can't enjoy them because of her endless string of worries.

Like, what if her mom needs her? What if she's sad? What if she eats raw chicken nuggets, or can't remember what channel the cupcake show is on, the show she and Violet watched five episodes of last night, even though Violet had homework to do?

Just call her and check, she tells herself, wanting to tear at her hair. *Yes, it's dumb, but you'll feel better afterward. Just use the office phone and call her.*

"Vi? Is that you hiding behind the corner, luv?" Mr. McGreevy says.

"Um, hi," she says. She hadn't intended for him to

see her yet. She hadn't thought he could see her yet, but apparently she was wrong.

"What can I do for you?"

She sighs. To use the phone, she has to have permission, but she feels weird asking. She does step closer, though.

Mr. McGreevy swivels away from his computer. "Aren't you supposed to be outside? Or did the weather turn dreakit?"

Violet has no clue what "dreakit" means. It must be one of his odd non-American expressions. It has a dark and gloomy sound to it, though, and Violet wonders if perhaps she herself is *dreakit*, and she just didn't know the word for it until now. "Um, I don't think so. But . . . can I use the phone, please? To call my mom?"

"Dunno why not." He pushes the phone across the desk, lifts the receiver, and presses 9. He hands the receiver to her and says, "All yours, luv."

Violet pushes in her own telephone number, all the while wishing the phone was all hers, and that Mr. McGreevy would go make coffee or something. But no, he stays put, typing away and murmuring the occasional phrase beneath his breath.

"Crikey," he mutters, for example. "Must call Revolution Foods. Order's due this afternoon."

"Hello?" Violet's mom says on the other end of the line.

"Mom! Hi!" Violet says. Mr. McGreevy glances up, and Violet turns sideways. "Um . . . so how *are* you?"

"Violet?" her mom says. "Aren't you supposed to be at school?"

"I am at school." She lowers her voice. "I just wanted to check on you."

"*Check* on me? Why?"

Violet ducks down as far as the cord will let her. *Because I love you? Because I'm worried about you? Because I don't want to be worried about you?* None of these answers will do. "Did you eat breakfast?"

"Violet. Boo."

Don't call me Boo, not when I'm at school, Violet thinks as her eyes tear up.

"Go back to class, baby."

"I'm not in class. I'm outside."

"They have a telephone outside?"

This remark could be funny, but today it's not. Not to Violet. "No, everyone else is outside. I'm inside. I just . . ." She closes her eyes. "Never mind."

"I don't know what to tell you, Boo," her mom says. "You've got to trust that I'm all right, and that I can take care of myself." She laughs. "I don't need you checking in on me during playground time, for heaven's sake."

Recess, Mom, Violet thinks. *Not playground time.* "You're right," she says abruptly. "I'm going back to *playground time*. Bye."

She has to straighten up in order to hang up the phone. When she does, she sees Mr. McGreevy studying her. Fantastic.

"All's well at home?" he says. "Everything shipshape and Bristol fashion?"

"I have no idea what that means," she tells Mr. McGreevy, starting back toward the playground.

"You're ribbing me," Mr. McGreevy says, projecting his voice. "'Shipshape and Bristol fashion'? You've never heard that?"

Violet halts. You can't just walk away from a teacher,

even if he isn't a real teacher but a secretary or an administrative assistant or whatever. She turns and says, neutrally, "Nope, that's a new one for me." She realizes she's curled her hands into fists, and she hides them behind her. "I'm going back outside, okay?"

"Then again, perhaps *shipshape* isn't a term much used by the ladies," Mr. McGreevy muses. He taps his chin. "What might a girl say in its place, hmm?"

A girl, if she weren't raised with good manners, might say that she didn't care in the slightest. An ill-mannered girl might go so far as to suggest that *no one* uses the term *shipshape*, whether male, female, or a talking teacup.

Mr. McGreevy snaps his fingers. "Tickety-boo! That's it! That's what me mum said when I was a boy." He adopts a falsetto. "'Everything tickety-boo, lad?'" He pretends to be an aggrieved grade school student. "'Yes, Mum. Tickety-boo. I'm going back to my models now, right?'"

Violet ducks her head. Mr. McGreevy was a boy once, and he made models. *Of what*, she wonders? Boats? Planes? Cars?

"Violet ...," he says.

His voice is gentler than before, and she braces

herself, because here it comes. Whatever it is—words of sympathy or a well-meaning reminder to keep her chin up—here it comes.

"It's a mum's job to be a mum," he says.

"Uh...what?"

"Even when they're irritating as all get-out. Even when you're at the end of your tether, and you think no one's got it worse than you."

No one does have it worse than me, Violet thinks.

"But that's the beauty of it, see?" Mr. McGreevy says. "It's not your job to smother your mum by checking in on her and the like. It's her job to smother *you*."

Violet holds herself still. She tries not to breathe, even. "But...what if she can't?"

"But she *can*. You're the kid, not the parent. That's what makes it so brilliant. *Your* job is to love your mum, and mind her, but that's all there is to it, really."

Tears flood Violet's eyes, surprising them both. Violet is horrified, and Mr. McGreevy winces.

"Ah, great," he says. "I've put my foot in my bloody mouth, haven't I?"

Violet blinks rapidly. "Can I go back to recess?"

"Of course. Go, go! Begone, you scurvy lass!"

Violet starts off. Then she stops, staring at the carpet. She wants to tell him she's not a scurvy lass, because that's what a normal girl would say. She also wants to tell him thank you, kind of.

"Listen, you," he says, sparing her the trouble. "It's all going to be tickety-boo, you hear?"

She looks back at him from over her shoulder. She gives him the best smile she can muster. "Right. And also shipshape and . . . and—"

"Bristol fashion," he supplies.

"Yeah. That."

❊ Eleven ❊

Yasaman's *ana* picks her up after school, along with Nigar. Her *ana* is unusually quiet, but Nigar fills the silence with her report of the day. Her words form a bubbling, never-ending stream of joy, and Yaz smiles, because it wasn't always this way. At the beginning of preschool, some of Nigar's classmates— two boys, in particular—teased Nigar about her name and about the way she looked.

But Nigar is over that now, and she's blessed with a little person's ability to truly forget, forgive, and move on.

Today, it seems, Nigar moved on using one of her favorite forms of locomotion: *hopping.*

"We were galloping kangaroos," she tells Yasaman and her mother from her booster seat in the back. "We were galloping kangaroos, and do you know what we called ourselves? We called ourselves The Galloping Kangaroos!" She breaks into a peal of giggles.

Yaz glances at her mom, ready to share a smile.

"That's clever," Yasaman's *ana* said, distracted.

"I was the leader," Nigar proclaims proudly, "so I got to boss everyone around. 'Jump, jump, jump!' I said." She bounces in her booster seat. "'Now dig! Dig, dig, dig!' Kangaroos love to dig. Did you know that, Yazzy?"

"I did," Yasaman says, twisting to grin at Nigar. She turns back. "*Ana?* Are you all right?"

Her mother doesn't reply. She opens her mouth as if she might, then closes it when Nigar continues with her kangaroo update. She could have spoken on top of Nigar, though. In a house—or a minivan—with an almost-four-year-old in it, the older people pretty much have to talk over the four-year-old if they ever want to get a word in.

Troubled, Yasaman sits back in her seat. *Katie-Rose called that girl, Josie,* she reminds herself. *Ana's not worried about that. Anyway, does everything in the world revolve around Yasaman? No.*

"And then we were galloping kangaroos with sticks!" Nigar exclaims. "So I said, 'Now pick up sticks, everyone! Now gallop, gallop, gallop!'"

Yaz lets Nigar's silliness wash over her. She's proud of her little sister for being so free and wild and bold, even as a galloping kangaroo with sticks. Yasaman, when she was in preschool, was never a galloping kangaroo with sticks. She mainly swung a lot, or sat by herself in one of the plastic playhouses.

When they get home, Yaz takes off her *hijab*, folds it up neatly, and shakes out her hair. *Ahhh.* Then she says, "Do you want help with dinner, *Ana?*"

"No, no," her mother says. "Do your homework. I'll take care of dinner."

"Um . . . okay," Yaz says, even though her *ana* doesn't like the word *um* or the word *okay*. Her *ana* would prefer Yasaman speak more properly than that.

Yaz retreats quietly from the kitchen with her

schoolbooks, taking them outside. Nigar is outside, too, galloping around like a galloping kangaroo. Her bows are pink today, to match her pink jeggings. Pink jeggings! Yasaman would never have been allowed to wear pink jeggings when she was Nigar's age.

She shouldn't complain. Hulya, Yaz's older cousin, has given Yaz some awesome hand-me-downs (which Nigar calls handy-downs), including black skinny jeans and a black-and-white *hijab* that matches the jeans perfectly.

Yaz settles down by her beloved butterfly bush, tucking her legs beneath her. The bush is now out of its pot and fully and officially planted in the soil of the yard, and just looking at it makes her feel blessed. It's her butterfly bush. Hers! A friendship gift, which is the best kind.

A yellow butterfly alights on a purple blossom. Its wings are tissue-thin.

"Hi, butterfly," Yaz whispers. "Is it fun being a butterfly? It is, isn't it?"

"Yee-haw!" Nigar shouts as she loops past.

Yaz smiles. "Where did you learn 'yee-haw,' Nigar?"

"My boyfriend, Damien!" Nigar shouts as she gallops past. "Only he is not really my boyfriend! He is Lucy's boyfriend, but sometimes we share, and sometimes I am their baby. Or their cat. *Yee-haw!*"

Yasaman is amused at the idea that her little sister has a sometimes-boyfriend-sometimes-owner. Katie-Rose would be appalled, and thinking about that amuses Yasaman, too.

Yasaman opens her *Wordly Wise* book, but she doesn't look at it. She watches the yellow butterfly instead. She remembers learning at some point in her life that a butterfly's life span is short, that they live for just one day or maybe two. *So sad*, Yaz thinks. Still, that one day—or two—must be glorious.

She sighs and starts her homework. Sometime later, her mother calls, "Yasaman? Come in now, please. Your *baba* is home, and he and I would like to talk to you."

Her *ana* and *baba* want to talk to her? Why? Shakily, she stands.

"Yee-*haw!*" Nigar cries, circling around once more.

Yasaman finds her parents in the living room. Out of all the rooms in their house, the living room feels the least homey, which is ironic since it's called the *living* room. Her parents are sitting on the pale blue sofa that

doesn't have a single stain on it. Their expressions are ...
hard to read. Not happy, though. Definitely not happy.

She crosses the plush carpet. Rather than squishing
into the sofa with them, she sits in the nearby armchair.
Her mouth is dry. "Yes?"

"Your *ana* got an interesting call today," her father says.
Yasaman's parents share a glance. "From a ... Josie Sanders?"

Yasaman closes her eyes. *Katie-Rose, what did you do?*
she thinks. *Or rather, what* didn't *you do?* Because Katie-
Rose promised up and down and side to side over her
heart that she talked to Josie and said to take Yasaman's
name off the trapeze class list. She swore to this a million
times over the course of the day, starting in their morning
art class and keeping it up until their very last class.

During math, she wrote notes and tossed them onto
Yasaman's desk. She whispered, "You believe me, right?"
when they were copying vocabulary words, and during
lunch, she said, "I am making a cross over my heart *right
now*. Do you see? Do you see me making this cross? And
I'm not even Catholic! But that's how much you can trust
me when I tell you that I have taken care of everything!"

And Yasaman did. She did trust her.

Now Katie-Rose's earnestness smacks of desperation, and Yasaman feels the cold weight of a stone in the pit of her stomach.

"This Josie, she said you wanted to take . . . trapeze lessons?" Yasaman's *ana* says. "She said she visited your school, and the children, they turned in their names if they wanted to participate?"

Yasaman is miserable. She twists her hair around her fingers.

"She was surprised you hadn't told me," Yasaman's mother says. She frowns. "I, too, was surprised."

Yasaman's *baba* takes her mother's hand. "Would you like to explain, Yasaman?"

To Yasaman's dismay, she bursts into tears. She tells her parents everything—well, *almost* everything—and ends with, "And Katie-Rose, she called Josie and took my name off the list! She promised!"

"Let me get this straight," Yasaman's father said. "Katie-Rose filled out a . . . what, a sign-up sheet? She filled it out with your name?"

"She filled one out with her name, too," Yasaman hastens to add. "She's really really really excited about the trapeze classes, and she knew her parents would say yes. She wanted me to sign up, too, but I told her no."

She takes a quivery breath. "And when I found out that she signed me up anyway, I *told* her to call the teacher. You have to believe me."

"I do believe you, Yasaman," her *baba* says. "You've never given me reason not to." Yasaman's relief is short-lived, as the next words out of his mouth are, "But as for Katie-Rose . . . I'm not pleased with what I'm hearing. Yes, Katie-Rose is an energetic child. That, I know. I assumed she was a person of strong character, however."

Yasaman's tears start anew. "She is! She just . . . she just . . ." Hopelessness descends over her, because what can she say to make her *baba* understand? Muslim families are different from non-Muslim families. Or, no. That's too easy. Yasaman's family is different than Katie-Rose's family, because there are strict and less-strict parents in every religion. Yasaman is sure.

On top of that, Katie-Rose's parents wouldn't be pleased to find out their daughter had forged Yasaman's name, either. Their reaction might not be as strong as Yasaman's father . . . or then again, it might.

"Please don't be mad at Katie-Rose," Yasaman says. She stares at her legs, too ashamed to meet his gaze. "Please?"

There is murmuring between her parents.

"Hmm," she hears her *baba* say, as if to express again his disapproval. But he leaves—Yasaman hears him stand and go out of the room—and then her *ana* is beside her, brushing away her tears.

Yasaman sniffles and lifts her head.

"*Küçüğüm,*" her *ana* says, which in English means "my sweet girl."

"Is *Baba* going to make me stop being friends with Katie-Rose?" Yasaman says.

Her *ana* shakes her head. "No, Yasaman. Everybody makes mistakes. And Katie-Rose didn't act out of malice, did she?"

"No, never. She just … doesn't think sometimes, that's all."

Her *ana* perches next to Yasaman on the armchair. She strokes Yasaman's long, glossy hair. Yasaman's heart is still thumping, but not as frantically as before. She gulps and takes a shuddery breath.

"When I was a girl, I played soccer," her *ana* says.

"In Turkey, we called it football. Did you know that, Yasaman?"

Yasaman is stunned. Her *ana* played soccer? Her *ana* ran around a field chasing a ball, possibly even kicking it?

"I went to an all-girls school, of course," her *ana* continues. She smiles. "I was quite good. Very fast."

Yasaman can't wrap her head around her mother's story. She has only seen her *ana* in skirts and stylish slacks suitable for a wife and mother. At her all-girls school, when she was young, did she play soccer in slacks?

"Rivendell is not an all-girls school," her *ana* says.

Yasaman knows that, of course. She waits on pins and needles to hear what her *ana* will say next.

"I asked this *Josie* if the trapeze class would be just for girls. She said no."

Yasaman exhales. She was holding her breath without realizing it, and now she feels . . . deflated.

"But Yasaman, my beautiful daughter, you are ten years old. A ten-year-old is a child, not yet a young lady. Not yet a woman." She lowers her hand and cups Yasaman's cheek. "Do you want to take this . . . *trapeze* class, Yasaman?"

"No?" Yasaman says uncertainly.

Her *ana* tilts her head.

Yasaman gathers her courage. "Y-yes?"

"You want to fly through the air with the greatest of ease?" her *ana* says, a liveliness dancing in her eyes.

Yasaman can't believe this is happening. She's not quite sure what *is* happening. What her *ana* just said rings a bell, though. Yasaman received a CD as a birthday present, a collection of children's songs, and one of them was about a trapeze artist in the circus. She hasn't thought of that song in ages.

"I do," Yasaman says, and her yearning hits her with full force. She *does* want to fly through the air. She wants to so much.

Her *ana* grows serious. "Your *baba* has reservations. But as I said, you're ten years old, not fifteen. It is fine for you to do an after-school activity with boys. You're in classes with them all day long, yes?"

Yes, yes, she *is* in classes with them all day long. She bobs her head, and her hair bounces against her shoulders. Her long hair, which is usually covered and bound. Her excitement ebbs.

"But … what about my *hijab*?" she asks. Trapeze lessons

will involve, among other things, hanging upside down. Her underwear will *not* show, as Katie-Rose wondered out loud, because she'll be wearing pants. But how can Yasaman hang upside down in her *hijab*? It will slip out of place. It will expose her hair. It will mess everything up!

"Stay here," Yasaman's *ana* says, patting Yasaman's knee and rising. She leaves the living the room, and a l-o-n-g time passes before she returns, carrying a cloth-wrapped package. She places it in Yasaman's lap.

Yasaman looks at it, then at her mother.

"Open it," her mother says.

Yasaman peels back the folds of cloth. Within, folded into a neat bundle, is more cloth. She lifts up this second piece of cloth. It's made out of stretchy material, and unlike a conventional *hijab*, it can't be unfolded into the shape of a scarf. It can't be unfolded at all. Yasaman examines it from all angles. It's somewhat like a ski mask, but with one big face-size hole instead of holes just for your eyes, and with fabric trailing beyond where a ski mask would end.

"You pull it over your head," her mother says. Her voice is animated. "Try it."

Yasaman does as she's told, twisting and tugging until her head pops through the opening.

"It's not the most flattering *hijab*, but it stays in place, see?" her mother says.

Yasaman shakes her head. The flowing ends of the *hijab* whip about, but the part framing her face stays put. She gets to her feet and does jumping jacks, and then twirls, and then as much of a backbend as she's capable of. She comes out of the backbend breathing hard. She realizes she'll have to put her hair in a ponytail and tuck it inside the stretchy ski mask part, but that's no big deal. For her final test, she just leans over with straight legs and touches her toes. Her head hangs low. The strange new *hijab* remains in place.

She stands up, beaming. "I can go upside-down."

"Indeed. Modesty is important, but Allah gave you your strong body for a reason."

Yasaman's spine tingles. "So . . . does this mean . . . ?"

"The answer is *yes*, Yasaman. Yes, you can take the trapeze class." Her *ana* smiles and cups Yasaman's cheek, blessing her in the traditional Muslim way. "*Bismillah ar-Rahman ar-Rahim.*"

❋ Twelve ❋

Camilla

MarshMilla:	yaybies! yr online!
The*rose*Knows:	of course I'm online. I'm editing my film from art class, which I'm thinking I'll call . . . drumroll, please . . . *The Mighty Wind of Doom!!!*
The*rose*Knows:	do u luv it, or do u luv it?
MarshMilla:	hmm. I love it and am disgusted by it in the same amount.
The*rose*Knows:	no, u luv it. my next film will prolly be from trapeze class, which starts tomorrow, altho I might not bring my camera

	tomorrow since I might need, you know, a few lessons before I'm really good.
The*rose*Knows:	I *still* can't believe you're not taking it, btw.
MarshMilla:	but u definitely are? the girl who's teaching the class called your parents, and they gave u permission?
The*rose*Knows:	yeppers! and her name's Josie. and my parents think it'll be a "good way for me to get rid of excess energy," whatever that means.
MarshMilla:	oh. okay.
MarshMilla:	so, um, did u know that Josie called yaz's parents, too?
The*rose*Knows:	WHAT? 😨
MarshMilla:	uh-huh. I just this second got off the phone with yaz. she's pretty upset.
The*rose*Knows:	oh crud! oh crud in a can!
MarshMilla:	yeah, she said her parents were all, "yasaman, would you sit down please? we need to talk." like, in scary parent voices.
The*rose*Knows:	crud!!!!! I'm so dead, aren't I? 💀 💀 💀

MarshMilla: it's pretty bad, I can't lie. yaz is being sent to an all-girls boarding school, and she's never allowed to have contact with u again. not that she wants to . . . altho who knows? maybe she'll come around in time, like in five or ten years or so.

The*rose*Knows: milla! this is terrible!!!! I SWEAR TO BOB I NEVER MEANT THIS TO HAPPEN!!!

The*rose*Knows: omigosh, what shld I do? shld I go to Yasaman's house and tell the Tercans it's all my fault?

MarshMilla: oh, they *know* it's yr fault. if I were u, I'd just . . .

MarshMilla: yikes, this is a hard one. I guess I'd just . . .

The*rose*Knows: what? tell me!!!!!

MarshMilla: *giggles*

The*rose*Knows: Milla!!!!! our best friend is getting sent to jail, and it's MY fault, and yr GIGGLING?

MarshMilla: *giggles some more*

MarshMilla: relax, katie-rose. i'm kidding!

The*rose*Knows: wait—what? yaz isn't getting sent to jail?

MarshMilla: she was never getting sent to jail. I never said that.

The*rose*Knows: and Josie never called her parents? OH THANK YOU, GREAT CHEEZE PUFF IN THE SKY! omigosh, Milla, u scared the crap out of me!!!!

MarshMilla: hold on. josie DID call, but by a wonderful miracle, it all turned out ok. yaz said that she and her mom talked, and it was a good talk. and yr never gonna believe it, but they're going to let her take the class. 🥴

The*rose*Knows: really?

MarshMilla: really.

The*rose*Knows: REALLY?!!

MarshMilla: really! 🐰

The*rose*Knows: whoa. that's the awesomest awesome sauce ever! and, um, Yaz isn't mad at me? +smiles hopefully+

MarshMilla: oh, no, she's plenty mad. she sez she'll only forgive u if you get yr booty in gear and help with Project Teacherly Lurve.

The*rose*Knows: what? but I don't wanna!

MarshMilla: that's why u have to. u owe it to her.

MarshMilla: anyway, just admit it. Mr. E and Ms. P wld be so cute together!

The*rose*Knows: wait a sec, lady. did Yaz say "Katie-Rose has to help or I'll never forgive her," or did u make that up on yr own?

MarshMilla: does it matter? u need to be supportive even if u "don't wanna." think about it, katie-rose. think HARD. when has yaz ever not been supportive of something u wanted?

The*rose*Knows: erm . . . when I signed her up for trapeze lessons? 🙂

MarshMilla: +rolls eyes+

The*rose*Knows: aarrrgh. fine. I'll be supportive (gag barf vomit 🤢), altho I wld like it noted that I see no reason for us to waste our time with stupid love problems NOW when we'll have to deal with them soon enuff anyway. like when we're oldheads and have to get married and wear stupid wedding dresses. BLECH! 😝

MarshMilla: this is u being supportive? wow.

The*rose*Knows: we're in 5th grade! 5th grade is where a kid can be a kid!!!!

MarshMilla: omg, are u quoting the Chuck E. Cheese's commercial at me? I *hate* Chuck E. Cheese's. my Mom Joyce does, too. when I was little and I got invited to a Chuck E. Cheese's b-day party, Mom Joyce always made Mom Abigail take me. she'd be like, "I can't. I can't do it. There's never any windows in those places, and that giant rat creeps me out— especially when it sings."

The*rose*Knows: he's a *he*, not an *it*, and he's a *mouse*.

MarshMilla: right. and that makes it so much better because . . . ?

The*rose*Knows: oh shut up. I said I'll be supportive about Project Stupid-in-Love, so I will, okay? only what am I supposed to do?

MarshMilla: not call it that, for starters. and I dunno, come up with an actual plan for getting Mr. E and Ms. P together. u can do that, k-r. you're smart.

The*rose*Knows: true

MarshMilla: yaz and I found out that they both like cookies and stuff, especially if they're homemade, so tomorrow I'm going to bring Mr. Emerson a plate of my Mom Abigail's brownies and tell him to share with Ms. Perez. what do u think of that?

The*rose*Knows: u shld only bring him one. it can be a big one, but then they'll have to break it in half, which is more lovey-dovey (gag barf vomit) then holding out a plate and saying, "here, want a brownie?"

MarshMilla: see? BRILLIANT. but did u quit with the gagging and barfing and vomiting?

The*rose*Knows: but I like gagging and barfing and vomiting, and anyway, I can't help it. and anyway *again*, the brownie idea is decent, but if u want Project Stupid-in-Love to work, you're going to have to do more than that.

MarshMilla: we're going to have to do more, and I agree. so what do we do?

The*rose*Knows: they have to spend, like, quality time

together, and it can't be planning lessons or waiting in line for the copy machine.

MarshMilla: go on

The*rose*Knows: all right, well, what about the Lock-In?

MarshMilla: ???

The*rose*Knows: what if we get Ms. Perez to chaperone the Lock-In instead of Mrs. Gundeck?

MarshMilla: katie-rose, that's perfect! first of all, Ms. Perez is a zillion times cooler than Mrs. Gundeck. second of all, Ms. Perez and Mr. Emerson wld be with each other for 4 whole hours, and they'd be the only grown-ups there. plus they'd be doing fun stuff, not teacher stuff. and third of all . . . pajamas!

MarshMilla: trading Mrs. Gundeck for Ms. Perez is the best plan ever. but how?

The*rose*Knows: I dunno. how am I supposed to know?

MarshMilla: cuz u just are. cuz it's *your* plan.

The*rose*Knows: well, I'll have to think about it. genius like mine cannot be forced.

The*rose*Knows: I cld call Chrissy, I guess . . .

MarshMilla: chrissy, yr babysitter?

The*rose*Knows: I prefer the term "older companion," but yes.

MarshMilla: why wld u call her?

The*rose*Knows: cuz she knows things

The*rose*Knows: then again, there are times when she totally doesn't. like, I asked her what it means if a boy farts in yr face, and u wanna know what she said?

MarshMilla: by "a boy," do u mean preston?

The*rose*Knows: no, and nvm. forget I mentioned it.

MarshMilla: c'mon, tell me. u know u want to, or u wldn't have brought it up.

The*rose*Knows: WRONG. I brought it up *accidentally*, and what Chrissy said was just plain dumb.

MarshMilla: dumb, huh? think u cld give me a *teensy* bit more detail? pretty please with a cheese puff on top?

The*rose*Knows: UGH. fine, she said mumble mumble mumble

MarshMilla: come again?

The*rose*Knows: I said she said mumble mumble mumble,

but clearly she was just trying to get my goat.

MarshMilla: get your . . . ?

MarshMilla: omigosh! chrissy said he likes u, didn't she!

The*rose*Knows: NO

MarshMilla: *preston likes katie-ro-ose! preston likes katie-ro-ose!*

The*rose*Knows: SHUT. UP.

MarshMilla: ooo-la-la, there might be LOTS of matchmaking going on at the Lock-In, even more than we thought! 🧸💟

The*rose*Knows: I *said* shut up! and fyi, he's not even coming.

MarshMilla: he's not? well, maybe while u figure out how to get Ms. P to take Mrs. G's place, I'll work on getting preston to change his mind. whaddaya think?

The*rose*Knows: I think NO. I think that's the most terrible idea ever, and if u *do*, I'll . . . I'll . . . I'll barf all over u, *and* gag *and* vomit!

MarshMilla: you're embarrassed! that's so adorable!

MarshMilla: night-night, my flower friend. sleep tight, don't let the bedbugs bite . . . and dream of sweet preston all thru the night!

 MarshMilla

hi! I'm supposed to be in bed, but I'm too excited because
of Katie-Rose's EXCELLENT idea for Project Teacherly Lurve.
We still have some kinks to work out, but basically, here it
is: WE GET MS. PEREZ TO CHAPERONE THE LOCK-IN INSTEAD OF
MRS. GUNDECK!

 MarshMilla

It's brilliant! It's awesometatiousful, as Katie-Rose would
say! We just have to, ya know, figure out how to make
the switcheroo happen. That's easy, tho, right? Kinda?
Sorta?

 MarshMilla

But, um, there's something else I want to say, and
I'm a little nervous about it, which is why I'm saying
it here.

 MarshMilla

It has to do with Elena.

MarshMilla

There's no reason you all would know this, but I'm pretty
upset about how Modessa and Quin are trying to make

her part of their group. Because Elena is not evil! She should not be an *evil chick*, which is the most ridiculous thing I've ever heard of, and anyway, shouldn't Elena *like* chickens? Since she lives on a farm?

 Mar🍄shMilla

Okay, I'm getting off track. The point is, I know that Project Teacherly Lurve is our BIG project, but . . . well . . .

 Mar🍄shMilla

I feel like I need to add Elena into the mix, too.

 Mar🍄shMilla

Like I should warn her about Modessa and Quin's true identities, you know? And help her escape from their clutches?

 Mar🍄shMilla

So that's what I'm going to do. I've said it out loud—okay, typed it out loud—and that makes it official.

 Mar🍄shMilla

That's all, I guess. Except don't worry, Yaz. Like I said, Project Teacherly Lurve is our main focus, and I'm *totally* psyched about it. Totally, totally, totally.

MarshMilla

I just want to save Elena, too.

🌼🌼🌼🌼🌼🌼🌼🌼🌼🌼🌼🌼🌼🌼🌼
🌼🌼🌼🌼🌼🌼🌼🌼🌼🌼🌼🌼🌼🌼🌼
🌼🌼🌼🌼🌼🌼🌼🌼🌼🌼🌼🌼🌼🌼🌼
🌼🌼🌼🌼🌼🌼🌼🌼🌼🌼🌼🌼🌼🌼

Thursday, October 20

✳ Thirteen ✳

Camilla

There is a song on YouTube that every kid in America is making fun of, it seems, because of how dumb the lyrics are. The song is all about saying, "Yay, Friday! Party time!" but the lyrics are basically a preschooler's lesson in the days of the week. Like, "Yesterday was Thursday, today is Friday, tomorrow will be Saturday . . ."

It goes something like that, and sure, Milla agrees that it's goofy. But! Today *is* Thursday, and tomorrow *is* Friday, and that means . . . the Lock-In!!! If Milla had a packet of Funfetti, she would sprinkle it through the air as she follows her class outside for lunch.

Milla does not and will not ever have a packet of Funfetti, however, at least not if her Mom Abigail has anything to say about it. Why? Because Funfetti only comes in boxed cake mixes, and Mom Abigail is strongly against boxed cake mixes. Boxed cake mixes go against her principles, and she can detect the particular fake flavor of a non-homemade cake after eating the tiniest nibble. Same with brownies from a mix, muffins from a mix, chocolate chip cookies from one of those plastic-wrapped logs in the refrigerated section of the grocery store . . . *any*thing.

So, no Funfetti for Milla, but that's what Mom Joyce would call a high-class problem, since it means that Mom Abigail keeps their house stocked with delicious home-made baked goods. Like brownies! Yay!

This morning, Milla packed not one, not two, but *three* of her Mom Abigail's homemade brownies in her lunch box. This morning, she offered one of the brownies to Mr. Emerson, but before she officially handed it over, she told him there was one condition he had to agree to. And if he didn't? No brownie.

"What's the condition?" Mr. Emerson said, eyeing the

Saran-wrapped goodie. He knew what a good cook Milla's mom was, and he knew that her specialities were baked goods because she's donated lots of them to bake sale fundraisers over the years.

"That you share it with Ms. Perez," Milla said. She jiggled it in her palm. "It's big, see? So you'll both still get a full brownie, basically."

Mr. Emerson chuckled. He raked his fingers through his hair and shook his head. "All right, Milla, tell me this: Why didn't you bring Ms. Perez one of her own?"

"Well, I was supposed to. That's the problem," Milla explained. "I totally promised I would, but I forgot, and so that's why I need you to help me out. 'Kay?"

He inhaled and opened his mouth as if to speak. Then he exhaled and chuckled. *Again.* "Sure," he said. "I would be delighted to share your mother's delicious brownie with Ms. Perez." He wiggled his fingers. "Now hand it over, please, ma'am."

The second brownie is for Elena. Milla plans to give it to her before the end of lunch. It'll be an icebreaker, and also a purely nice gesture, and hopefully it'll remind Elena that Elena herself is a nice person who does nice things. Maybe Elena hasn't been nice this week, but that's because Modessa and Quin have confused her.

Milla plans to un-confuse her, because she wishes someone had done that for her when she got sucked into Modessa's mean games. Elena, in Milla's way of looking at things, kind of *is* Milla, back when Milla was teetering between accepting Modessa's friendship (regardless of the cost) and staying clear of Modessa (regardless of the cost).

Saving Elena is Milla's chance to go back and save herself. It's her chance to prove to Modessa and Quin that she *is not that girl anymore*, while at the same time protecting Elena from getting hurt later on down the road. She just prays she doesn't wimp out.

Today's weather is nice, so the teachers are letting the kids eat lunch outside. Milla spots Violet at their favorite table, the one near the tetherball court. She waves to let Violet know she's seen her, but she doesn't yet head over. She has a pit stop to make first, a freaky and nerve-wracking pit stop. She pauses and scans the playground, giving herself a mental pep talk as she does.

You're not *going to wimp out*, she tells herself. *You're braver than you give yourself credit for! You're not small,*

either, even though you drew yourself that way in Sunday
school. So get over it, okay?

Telling someone—even herself—to "get over it" isn't
the sort of thing Milla would generally do. But given the
circumstances, it feels right. She *doesn't* want to be small,
or to see herself as small, or to be seen by others as small.

As for being brave, she wants to live up to the example
set by her flower friends, who have done so many brave
things it's hard to keep track of them all. Like Yasaman,
who, when pressed to the wall, held her chin high and told
her parents she *did* want to take trapeze lessons, despite
being scared to death of their reaction.

Like Katie-Rose, who can be a busybody, but who's certainly not afraid to do whatever she wants to do.

And like Violet, who is the bravest of them all, Milla
thinks. Her mom just got released from the locked ward of
California Regional's mental hospital. Violet *has* to be ter-
rified at the thought of her mom getting sick again, since
if she got sick again, she'd be locked up again. Talk about
scary! But Violet keeps pushing through it, staying strong
for her mom. Maybe *too* strong, a possibility Milla stores
away for later consideration.

She sees the back of Modessa's head. She's flanked by Quin on one side and Elena on the other, and Milla actually doesn't want to go over to them at all. The brownie, wrapped in Saran wrap and tied with a bow, dangles like dead weight from her hand.

But she has to go over to them, and so for courage, she replays a piece of advice her Mom Joyce gave her last night. She was having trouble falling asleep, and her mom asked why, and so Milla propped herself up on her elbow and told her a *little* bit of the Modessa-Quin-Elena story.

"Ah," her Mom Joyce said in that parent way of not actually saying "yes" or "no" to the story itself. She sat on Milla's bed and gentled Milla's elbow out of its propped-up position. Once Milla was lying down flat again, she said, "Milla, we all have fears. Every single person in the world has moments of being scared or nervous or whatever."

"Even you?" Milla asked.

Mom Joyce smiled. "Even me. But sweetie? You *can't* run away from the things that scare you, *especially* when you really really want to. Because if you do, do you know what'll happen?"

"What?"

"You'll experience a huge rush of relief, which your body will interpret as a reward. And by *rewarding* yourself for not doing the scary thing, you'll teach yourself to *keep* not doing the scary things."

"Oh," Milla said. It didn't sound *too* bad, rewarding yourself for not doing scary things.

Mom Joyce ran her fingers through Milla's hair the way Milla liked. "And Milla? The more you run away from things, or avoid certain situations, or say *no* to opportunities, the smaller your world becomes, until one day you wake up and find yourself in a tiny, walled-in box. Like Mrs. Krutcher from church. Do you remember Mrs. Krutcher?"

Milla knew of her, but she'd never met her, because she never came to the Sunday services. People at church called Mrs. Krutcher a "shut-in," and sometimes Pastor Sharon prayed for her during "Prayers for the People." There was a list of people who checked on her and brought her food on different days, and Mom Joyce and Mom Abigail were on that list, which made Milla proud.

"Well, you don't want to end up like her, not that you ever would," Mom Joyce finished. "But baby, believe me. That's not the life you want."

It isn't. Mom Joyce is right. A cool breeze lifts Milla's hair, reminding her of her mom's touch, and she squares her shoulders.

"Mills, over here!" calls Katie-Rose, who's joined Violet at their lunch table. She's wearing a T-shirt she probably stole from her dad's undershirt drawer, because it's huge on her. Across the front, in bold, handwritten letters, it says, CHICKS DON'T DIG STINKS.

Milla would smile if her stomach wasn't so knotted up.

Yasaman's there, too, looking far more elegant in jeans, a long-sleeved black shirt with a gold star in the middle, and a gold-flecked *hijab*. All three FFFs look at her curiously, and Katie-Rose hollers, "What's the hold up, lady?"

"One sec!" Milla calls. Because first? The brownie. Elena. Her heart thumps, but too bad. She makes her feet move forward.

When she's almost to them, Quin glances over her shoulder and sees her. Her eyes widen, and she turns back, speaking urgently to Modessa and Elena. Modessa cranes her neck to double-check Quin's report, maybe, and then there's more huddled-tight conversation. Quin laughs. Milla is all nerves.

They are just girls, Milla tells herself. *They. Are. Just. Girls.*

"Um, hi," she says when she's directly behind them.

In unison, they swivel to face her. Milla focuses on Elena, who gulps. She offers her the brownie, saying, "This is for you. You can, you know, share with Quin and Modessa if you want."

Elena doesn't accept it. Her chest rises and falls.

"*Remember*," Modessa warns her in a low voice.

"O-kaaay," Milla says. She shifts her weight. "So . . . can I speak to you alone?"

"No," Modessa says.

Milla looks at her. It must be a trick of the light, but her eyes are slanted, and she seems to have no pupils. "Is Elena not allowed to answer for herself? Are you afraid she'd say yes?"

"Whatever you want to say to Elena, you can say in front of all of us," Modessa says. "Right, Elena?"

Elena hesitates.

"Right, Elena?" Modessa repeats, and Elena startles and nods too vigorously.

"Fine," Milla says. She pretends that she's Mom Joyce, and she takes a seat by this doll-robot version of Elena that isn't really Elena, but just a human being with fears of her own. "Elena? Do you want to come to the Lock-In with me? I know you haven't signed up, but it's not too late."

Quin chokes back a laugh, but she wants Milla to hear. She wants Modessa to hear.

"We could go together," Milla presses on. "It'll be fun."

Elena grips the edge of the table. Her knuckles are white.

"Elena? Modessa isn't the boss of you." She tries to laugh in a way that shows how stupid Modessa is being. "You're allowed to talk to me if you want to."

"Oh, Camilla," Modessa says, as if whatever she's about to explain is a terribly easy concept to understand for all but the slowest students. "Elena knows what she's allowed to do and not do."

Milla feels heat rise to her face. She keeps her gaze on Elena. "Elena?"

"Is it time?" Quin asks, and Modessa must nod, because Quin says, "Three, two, one . . . now!"

All three girls bare their sharp, white teeth and hiss. Milla startles, jumping to her feet, but holding her ground. They've tried this trick once, and it worked, but it's not going to work again.

The three girls rise together and advance, and Milla's body tries to change Milla's mind. Milla's body wants to back away and run, because Modessa, Quin, and Elena are wolf-girls, witches, and evil chicks at the same time. They're just as likely to eat themselves as they are to eat Milla, and when Elena—*Elena!*—swipes the air with a claw-fingered hand, Milla loses all strength of will. She flees, their laughter chasing her as she runs from the table.

"*Milla*," someone says. "Milla, are you okay?"

Milla stops. Her breathing is labored. Max is looking at her with concern.

"H-hi," she says. She feels ashamed—did Max witness her encounter with the evil chick wolf-girls? Then she takes a big breath, lifts her chin, and tells herself, *No. You tried. Give yourself a little credit, at least.*

Max is still waiting for her answer

"Yeah, I'm totally okay. Well, not *totally*, but . . . um . . ." She bites her thumbnail. "I kinda went through something weird just now, but I'm fine." She makes a face to say that it's not worth talking about.

"Good," Max says. "Um, not about the weird thing, but good that you're okay, or fine, or whatever."

Milla gives him a small smile. He always seems to know how to make her feel better. She holds out the brownie Elena rejected and says, "Here, this is for you."

Max takes it. "Really? Cool."

Milla's mood lifts. She knows that Max will eat the brownie and think it's yummy, and that makes her feel almost happy. She expresses her almost-happiness by twisting her shoulders in a way that makes her skirt swish. She didn't know she knew how to do that, but it makes her feel cute. Flirty.

"You're welcome," she says. "Well . . . bye."

He touches her arm. "Hold on, I want to show you something." He glances around, and then, with his free hand, he unzips a pocket on his shirt. Milla is surprised, because until now she hadn't noticed that there *was* a pocket on his shirt.

She steps closer and sees that it's meant to be invisible, which is pretty cool. The shirt is black, the zipper is black, and not only that, the pocket isn't in a typical shirt-pocket location. It's higher up, and diagonal, so that it almost blends in with the shoulder seam.

Max glances at Milla, then pulls something out of the

invisible pocket. It's his iPhone, the one his parents gave him when his hamster died. He brought it to school even though he's not allowed! He reveals an inch of it before dropping it back into the hidden pocket and zipping the pocket shut.

"Omigosh!" Milla says.

"And not only that, but look." He fingers the collar of his shirt, and Milla sees that there are two small slits in the fabric, one on each side. From one of the slits, he tugs out an ear bud. "The other one's on the other side. The cord runs through the shirt and connects to my phone."

"That's awesome," Milla marvels.

"I wanted to show you, that's all."

"I'm glad."

"Maybe we can listen to music tomorrow night, at the Lock-In? If you want to?"

Milla imagines listening to music with Max, their heads close in order to share his headphones. "Yeah. Totally."

"Cool." He grins, and she holds that grin in her heart as she goes to join her friends. It's her reward for being brave.

❈ Fourteen ❈

After lunch, Katie-Rose stands up and brushes the Dorito crumbs from her jeans. She tightens first her right pigtail and then her left one.

"Excuse me, ladies, but I have some business to attend to," she announces. "I do hope you will forgive my absence and continue to chat pleasantly amongst yourselves until my return."

Her friends look at her.

"We'll try our best," Violet says.

"Where are you going?" Yaz asks. "What business do you need to attend to?"

"Simply that which needs to be done," Katie-Rose says grandly. She doesn't know what her sentence means, but she likes the sound of it. And so, on that note, she leaves.

Marching across the playground in her oversized shirt, she imagines that she's a general in war. Or, no. An Amazon! A fierce warrior, standing up for the rights of girls everywhere! Wonder Woman is an Amazon, she seems to recall. Although Wonder Woman wears a red bathing suit bottom with a blue star-spangled top, and no way in heck will Katie-Rose ever be seen in *that* get-up. Jeans and an oversized T-shirt is her superhero costume of choice. That's the way *she* rolls.

"Ahem," she says when she gets to the edge of the grassy field where kids play soccer. Preston is kicking the ball around with Chance, Brannen, and some other guys. They don't appear to notice her.

"Ah-*HEM*," she says again. The guys *still* don't notice her, so she marches right over to them, intercepting the ball and stepping on it with her sneaker.

"Katie-Rose!" Chance groans. "You blocked my shot!"

"Quit yer bellyaching," she growls. She plants her

fists on her hips, having transformed—for reasons unbeknownst even to her—from Amazon warrior to gun-slinging cowboy. Wait, *girl*. Cow*girl*. "I have no beef with you." She jerks her chin at Preston, "It's your pardner I need to have words with."

She glares, determined to show no weakness. But on the inside, she's mortified. *Pardner? Really? Did I really just say* pardner?

Preston cocks his head, reading her shirt. "'Chicks don't dig stinks?'"

"That's right," she says. "And now might I have a moment of your time?"

"Ooo-ooo," Chance says in the foolish way of suggesting that romance is afoot.

"Shut up, Chance," she tells him. Anyway, who is he—the boy with seventeen girlfriends—to talk?

A smiles plays at Preston's lips, and he saunters toward Katie-Rose. "What's up?"

"I'll tell you in private," she says.

"Fine," he says, heading for the fence that surrounds the playground.

"Fine," she counters, heading there faster. No way

is *she* following *him*. She needs to be in *front* of him, in accordance with natural order as she perceives it.

They reach the fence at the same time. Katie-Rose stares Preston down—or tries to. He seems to be enjoying himself, the rat.

"You noticed my shirt, I noticed," she says.

"Ah," Preston replies. "Yes. I noticed you noticing my noticing."

"I know, because *I* noticed you noticing me noticing you."

"Are you sure? Because though I noticed you noticing my noticing, I did *not* notice you noticing me noticing you noticing me."

Katie-Rose attempts to play back his sentence in her head. She scowls. "Oh, shut your face."

He grins.

"What you need to know is that I am wearing this shirt on purpose," she says. "I am wearing this shirt, which I made myself—"

"*No*," he says, feigning astonishment. "*You* made that shirt? For real? Are you going to make more and sell them?"

"You better stop mocking me," Katie-Rose warns.

"Could you make one in pink, for my grandmom? Maybe add in some embroidery?"

She stomps on his toe.

"Ow!"

"I am wearing this shirt for one reason and one reason only: Because it is true, and because you are sadly, *sadly* mistaken if you think I can't handle grossness."

"That's two reasons," Preston says.

She stomps on his foot again.

"*Ow!*"

"I *said* shut your face!" she says sternly. But what is he doing? Is he laughing? Why is he laughing? It is very hard to maintain sternness when someone is laughing. For heaven's sake, doesn't he know that?

"*Preston*," she says in what she hopes is an intimidating voice.

He sobers up. "Yes, ma'am?"

"*Ha ha*. Now, listen. I can *handle* grossness fine. I just prefer not to, because it. Is. Gross. Do you understand?"

"You don't want to handle my grossness. Got it."

A sound comes out of Katie-Rose that could be

mistaken for a laugh, or if not a laugh, then a goat bleating. She tries to make her mouth behave, but the corners of her lips curve up defiantly.

"Stop!" she cries, addressing herself *and* Preston. "When we were in art, you said I was like Mrs. Gundeck, which was very rude. If you don't take it back, I will have to kill you."

He holds up his hands. "You're not like Mrs. Gundeck! I take it back!"

"Good. Now say, 'Katie-Rose is not scared of barf.'"

"Katie-Rose is not scared of barf."

She leans back on the fence. "Now say, 'Katie-Rose is un-gross-out-able, unlike Mrs. Gundeck.'"

"Katie-Rose is un-gross-out-able, which isn't even a word."

Katie-Rose doesn't correct him. Instead, she bounces forward off the fence she just leaned back against and grabs Preston by the shoulders. "Omigosh, I have just had *the* most genius idea in the history of the multiverse."

"The multiverse? What's a multiverse?"

"Preston, this is important, so *don't* lie. Can you make stinks on purpose? For real?"

"Why do you want to know?"

"*Can* you? And can you do it today, during German?"

"Maybe, but only if you tell me why."

Katie-Rose is too excited to bother with *whys.* "Because I owe someone a favor. You wouldn't understand."

He twists out of her grasp and turns to leave. "Then no. Sorry."

Aargh! She grabs his arm and whirls him back around. "All right, I'll tell you." She scans the playground until she spots Yasaman, her face framed by her golden *hijab.* Yaz genuinely wants Mr. Emerson and Ms. Perez to fall in love, and Katie-Rose genuinely wants Yaz to be happy. She thinks she may have found a way to make all of that happen: for Mr. Emerson, for Ms. Perez, and especially for Yaz.

"I'm waiting," Preston says.

So Katie-Rose outlines the flower friends' plan to get Mr. Emerson and Ms. Perez to become a couple. She knows he'll think it's silly and girlish, but she doesn't let that deter her.

"If you can fart during German, and it's anything like your farts from art, then you can stage a massive gross-out," she says. "If you can make just one person throw up, or if you can make Mrs. Gundeck *think* someone's going to throw up, then Violet can plant the idea that there's a virus going around. Violet's in your German class, right?"

"Yeah," Preston says. The wind ruffles his hair, and Katie-Rose catches a whiff of something sweet, like papaya or passion fruit. She sniffs again. Like her mom's Papaya Passion Punch Shampoo, with its "refreshing blend of papaya and tropical passion fruit that invigorates your senses and gives you a taste of paradise."

Does Preston use girly, yummy-smelling shampoo? Is that possible?

"I don't get how making Mrs. Gundeck think there's a throwing-up virus going around will help Mr. E and Ms. P in the romance department, though," Preston says.

In the romance department. Katie-Rose thinks that's sort of cute, at least until she remembers who said it.

"Because then Mrs. Gundeck won't want to chaperone the Lock-In, and Ms. Perez can step in," Katie-Rose explains. "And then . . . well, I don't exactly know. But Mr. Emerson and Ms. Perez will get to spend the whole night together."

He smirks. "Oh, yeah. The Lock-In."

"Yes, Preston, the Lock-In," she says. "I know you think it's stupid. I know you're *waaaaay* too cool to go to a school-sponsored event on a Friday night, but guess what? *I* know it's going to be awesome, so deal with it."

Preston looks at her, but Katie-Rose can't read his expression. Katie-Rose liked it better when they were laughing, but whatever. Laughing with Preston was a fluke. She knows that.

"So will you or not?" Katie-Rose says. She folds her arms over her chest and stares at him, but not directly into his eyes. She stares at a spot right *above* his eyes and hopes he won't be able to tell the difference.

"Sure," Preston says.

"I'm sorry . . . what?"

"The gross-out thing. Sure. I have German next, and as I just ate a healthy lunch, it should be no problem."

He belches, and Katie-Rose automatically says, "*Gross.*"

"Isn't that what you want?" Preston says.

She feels a tumble of emotions. Preston's willingness to help confuses her, as does his ability to make her laugh. Like, genuinely laugh. But then he had to go and act scornful about the Lock-In . . . and that hurt her feelings.

Just as she didn't know Preston could make her laugh, she didn't know he had the power to hurt her feelings. She assumed that by making a point of actively disliking Preston, she'd protected herself from that. She thought *she* held all the power.

"Great. Thanks," she says, and with no further ado, she walks away.

❈ Fifteen ❈

After school, Yasaman goes to the girls' bath-room and switches her "day" *hijab* for the "sports" *hijab* her *ana* gave her. It's not the prettiest headscarf she's ever seen, but she doesn't care.

She turns her head back and forth, and her hair stays tucked in. She jumps up and down, and it still stays tucked in. She knew it would, though, because she practiced with it lots last night. So maybe she jumped up and down not to double-check the security of her *hijab*, but out of excitement.

She should be nervous, but she's not.

She should feel self-conscious about her new, different-looking hair scarf, but she doesn't. (Well, maybe a little, but she's not going to let a case of the jitters stop her from reaching for the stars, or, in this case, the ceiling tiles in the PE Room, which is where all the trapeze students are to meet.)

She strides down the hall, holding her chin up and her shoulders back. She slips into the PE room and joins the nine other fifth graders who signed up for the class, wiggling in between Becca and Katie-Rose. Everyone's taken their shoes off, so she kicks hers off, too. She fumbles for Katie-Rose's hand.

"…and since it's an introductory level course, we'll be working with a single trapeze," Josie is saying. She's barefoot, like the others, and she stands confidently on a wide gym mat she's spread across the floor. Her hand rests on a slim metal bar attached to two thick ropes. The ropes are secured with hooks and wire cable, and it looks as stable as Josie promised her *ana* it would be.

Josie keeps talking, and Yasaman listens, but at the same time, she soaks in every detail she can. The gleam of the bar, the blindingly white ropes, the anticipation popping and fizzing in Yasaman's chest until it feels as though her soul has no bounds, expanding to fill the room and beyond. She will remember this feeling forever.

Josie tells them what skills they'll learn—drops, balances, hangs—and as she speaks, she plays with the trapeze, pushing it gently so that it sways back and forth. Yasaman's pulse thrums. She can't wait to grip the fibers of the ropes, to perch on the bar, to experience at last what it's like to fly.

Josie catches the bar and holds it still. "So. Who wants to go first?"

Yasaman's hand shoots up. Some of the kids are surprised, she can tell. Yasaman wants to go first? Shy, quiet Yasaman?

"Fantastic, let's do it," Josie says.

Katie-Rose squeezes Yasaman's hand. Yaz squeezes back. She leaves the group, steps onto the squishy mat, and walks to Josie, where she mirrors Josie's stance by planting her feet about a foot apart. Josie passes her the trapeze, and Yaz catches the metal bar, which is the part that would be the "seat" if the trapeze was a swing.

"Step closer," Josie says, gesturing for Yaz to approach.

"Terrific. Now, turn so that your back's toward me ... yep ... and now I want you to let go of the bar with one hand and bring your other hand all the way to the end of the bar so that it's flush with the rope."

"Which hand should I hold on with?" Yaz asks.

"Either is fine, just—that's right." Josie glances at the class. "Check it out: Her knuckles are aligned, her wrist is straight, and the edge of her thumb is grazing the rope. That's the perfect form for the mount we're going to start with." She smiles at Yaz. "Great job ... um ..."

"Yasaman," the other kids fill in, like contestants in a game show. They sound proud of Yaz, proud that she's doing so well and proud that she's one of them. Warmth blooms in Yasaman's core and spreads all the way to her fingers, which are itching to do more, more, more.

"Great job, Yasaman," Josie says. "Now listen while I explain what you're going to do, please, and then you can give it a try. But learning to do tricks on the trapeze is a process, just like everything else in life. Don't worry if it takes a few tries."

Yasaman nods.

"So here's what's going to happen. You're going to

walk from one end of the bar to the other, sliding your hand with you. Then turn around, lean back, and swing your other hand up so that you're gripping the bar with both hands. Then kick one leg up and over the bar, while pushing off the ground with the other. It takes a bit of a jump. You have to commit."

Josie seems so serious. But then, Yasaman is, too. Serious and buzzing and totally ready to commit, as in now, before she has a chance to think too much about it.

"If you can get your leg over the bar, you've done the hardest part," Josie says. "Then hold on by bending your leg, like I'm sure you've done a thousand times on the monkey bars."

Yasaman doesn't respond, and she doesn't look at her classmates, either. She hasn't hung upside down from the monkey bars since she was Nigar's age, practically. Before she started wearing a *hijab*. But once upon a time she did hang upside down from the monkey bars, and she's almost a hundred percent sure she can do it again.

Or ninety-percent sure. Seventy-five percent sure? Okay, if she really really had to swear to it—not that she would, as she doesn't swear—she'd say she's fifty percent sure she'll be able to get her leg hooked over the bar, and thus fifty percent sure she won't end up flat on her back on the blue gym mat. A fifty-fifty chance, those are good odds!

"When your leg's holding the bar, you can grab the ropes and pull yourself up to sitting," Josie tells Yasaman. "Cool?"

"Cool," Yaz says.

Josie steps back, waving her hand in front of her to say, *The space is all yours.*

"Yay, Yaz!" Katie-Rose calls.

"You can do it!" Becca says.

Yaz visualizes the steps Josie explained, practicing in her mind what she's about to do. Her heart is a small thing with wings. It flutters.

Then she takes a deep breath, and then one more deep breath, and just . . . goes for it. With her right hand on the bar, she takes two steps forward. She pivots, leans back, and throws her left arm up, catching the bar with her hand. With her quads, she pushes off the mat, launching her right leg high into the air while allowing her shoulders and head to swing upside down in counterbalance.

She hooks the bar with her leg. She's got it! She's got it, and her *hijab* is still on! She grabs a rope in each hand and pulls herself to a seated position. She's not terribly graceful about it, and it's a little embarrassing to be straddling the bar with one leg dangling from each side, but who cares? A smile splits her face.

"That was awesome," Josie says. Behind her, the other kids clap and cheer, and now Yaz can look at them. Now she can grin at her meddlesome FFF, Katie-Rose, who got her into this in the first place.

"You're, like, a natural, and I'm not just saying that," Josie marvels. "Since you're up there, do you want to try one more move before someone else takes a turn?"

"Sure," Yasaman says.

Josie nods her approval. "All right. Draw your left leg over the bar so that both legs are in front of you."

It's a tight squeeze, wiggling her knee and leg through the gap between her upper body and the bar, but Yasaman does it. Without thinking, she bends and flexes both legs, making the trapeze move through the air like a swing.

"Fun, isn't it?" Josie says, her lips curving upward.

"Now the tricky part. Bend your right arm—yeah, keep your left arm rigid and push against that opposite rope— and pull both legs up so that they extend from your hips at a ninety degree angle. Straighten them, that's right. Pretend you're just sitting on the ground with your legs out in front of you."

Yasaman wobbles. "They're both on the same side of the rope," she says, wanting very much not to fall. "Is that okay?"

"Yep. Press your spine into the rope behind you and tighten your muscles. That'll help with your balance."

Yasaman frowns and instinctively shifts her weight, rotating her hips so that the bar digs into her outer thigh. Instead of sitting on the pretend ground with her legs out in front of her, she's lying sideways on the pretend ground, her legs stacked on top of one another.

"Perfect!" Josie cries. "Omigosh, you're almost there. Now just flip your grip on the rope by your head so you can let the other rope go."

"Let it go?" Yaz squeaks.

Josie strides over. "Um, okay, like this." She loosens Yasaman's fingers and shows her how to reorient her right hand so that the rope twines around her forearm like a snake. Then she puts her hand on Yasaman's lower back and pushes, guiding Yasaman to arch her spine. With her spine arched, Yasaman's legs have no choice but to press hard into the rope she's supposed to let go of.

"Oh," Yaz says.

She feels it now, how the tension of her quads will hold her in place. So she does what Josie said. She lets go of the rope with her left hand, and now she's a dangling sideways T, her arms spread wide and her strong, straight legs anchoring her to the bar.

The other kids must be holding their breath, or why else would the room be so hushed, the air crackling with anticipation? Then, wham! Everyone bursts into applause. Katie-Rose claps the hardest, cheering and whistling and being her overall spazzy self.

Momentum sends the trapeze swaying in a gentle half-circle. Yasaman's *hijab* spills gracefully past her shoulders and grazes the blue gym mat. Yasaman floats through the air—or rather, flies. Her fluttering butterfly heart soars.

❁ Sixteen ❁

A t home, Violet plops onto her bed. She's felt
jittery and tense for the last few days, she feels jittery
and tense today. She's sick of it. She's trapped in what
seems like a constant current of anxiety, and only rarely
does something in the outside world pull her out of it.

When that happens, she's grateful, even if the break
is only temporary. Like this afternoon in German class,
when Preston produced from his gastrointestinal system
a stench so foul, so vile, so . . . tangible, almost, in its presence, that poor Ava held her nose, covered her mouth, and
staggered to Mrs. Gundeck's desk.

"Your bucket," she gasped.

"*Heilandsack!*" Mrs. Gundeck cried. "*Nein, nein!*"

"Your bucket, your bucket!"

Mrs. Gundeck leapt from her seat, moving faster than Violet thought her stout teacher could. She grabbed the bucket from the corner of the room, and thrust it at Ava, who promptly vomited up what she had in her stomach, which wasn't much. Maybe she vomited up nothing, for all Violet knew, but she made the *sound*, for sure, and the sound of retching is almost equal in strength to the distinctive odor of barf.

"Ewww!" everyone cried, except for Preston.

Preston grinned. He repeated his act of stenchery.

"*Prethton!*" Natalia wailed. "You know I am very thenthitive to all thingth crath!"

"Crap?" Thomas said. "You're sensitive to crap?"

The boys loved this, of course, and there were guffaws all around.

"*Crath,*" Natalia insisted. "Not crap. *Crath.*"

Preston feigned horror, drawing his hand to his face and widening his eyes. "You said crap, Natalia!"

"Pleathe! Crap ith crath, and I would never thay thomething tho … tho …"

Even Cyril, a ten-year-old boy version of Eeyore, moves his lips in an upward sort of twist. Violet, who feels a special affinity for Cyril because of his outcast status, caught his eye and smiled, and his lip quirk turned into a full-on smile. Cyril feels a special affinity for Violet, too, she's pretty sure. No, she's more than sure, and to claim otherwise would be coy. Violet doesn't like *coy*. Coy is for girls like Modessa and Quin. Coy is for anyone who wants to play games with people and their emotions instead of just saying, "Yes, I like you," or "No, I'm not having a great day, actually." Or "It's hard for me to relax, even in my own house. Especially in my house. It's hard for me … it's hard for me to be with my …"

It's hard to put in words, the thought Violet is dancing around. Dancing around a thought isn't the same as being coy, though. It's not fun. It isn't the same as playing games.

Violet closes her eyes. She's glad she made Cyril smile, because she *does* like Cyril. Not in a boy-girl way. She likes him because she senses that life isn't straightforward for him, just as life isn't straightforward for her. They share that knowledge of each other, that's all.

She's also glad Katie-Rose's crazy plan worked. Katie-Rose somehow persuaded Preston to fart on purpose—*???* how do boys *do* that?—in order to trigger a massive gross-out fest, and it worked. Grossness abounded, creating the perfect setup for Violet to act out her role in the passion play.

"I feel a little queasy, too, Mrs. Gundeck," she said, raising her hand and not waiting to be called on. "I've heard there's a stomach bug going around. A bad one."

"My dad said that, too," Preston said. "He's a doctor."

Preston's dad isn't a doctor. He's a repairman. Violet has seen him drop Preston off in a van that says, "Dwight's Home Service: Fixing Your Washing Machine So You Can Stay Clean."

"Well, I'm not thick," Natalia said, but everyone knew she meant "sick." "And I *refuthe* to *get* thick, becauthe tomorrow ith the Lock-In, and I *refuthe* to mith the Lock-In."

Preston frowned and tapped his chin. He probably thought it made him look doctorly. "Stomach bugs usually have an incubation period of twelve to twenty-four hours. So you'll either be fine *or* it'll hit you right when you get to The Lock-In." He gestured to include the rest of the class. "That's true for any of us who've been near Ava—no offense, Ava."

Ava clutched her bucket. She regarded Preston as if he was the slime coating a moldy sponge, but she couldn't find the energy to protest.

"Oh, man, wouldn't it suck if the Lock-In turned out to be a total barforama?" Preston continued.

Quin barked out a laugh. "*No.* It would be awesome! Only losers are going to the Lock-In, so I would be fine with it."

"Well, *I* wouldn't," Natalia said. "And you realithe you jutht called Mithith Gundeck a loother, don't you?" She switched into teacher's pet mode. "Becauthe Mithith Gundeck ith going to be there tomorrow night. Aren't you, Mithith Gundeck?"

By then, Mrs. Gundeck looked like she was considering a career change. Pale faced, she pointed to Ava. "You, go to the office." She pulled a Kleenex from the box on her desk and patted her forehead with it. "Actually, I'll walk you there—but *don't* breathe on me. I need to have a word with Ms. Westerfeld."

"About what?" Violet asked.

Mrs. Gundeck made her way unsteadily across the room, using desks along the way for support. "It has occurred to me that I double-booked myself for tomorrow night. I have bingo with my knitting circle tomorrow night. What was I thinking?"

What was she thinking, indeed? Violet thought, because her last-minute excuse didn't even make sense. Wouldn't a knitting circle get together to knit? Wouldn't a bingo group get together to play bingo?

But hey, it worked. Katie-Rose's nutty plan worked, and when Mrs. Gundeck returned from the office and dismissed class early, Violet cruised by the music room to give her the good news.

Preston, of all people, beat her to it. When Violet saw him outside the music room, she stopped short. He did a sneaky wave to get someone's attention, and then he grinned and gave a thumbs-up. From within the room came a high-pitched squeal.

"No way!" she heard Katie-Rose exclaim. Violet heard

her from the hall, and she also heard the music teacher scold Katie-Rose. Violet hurried off. She assumes Preston did, too.

There's a knock at Violet's door, and Violet's eyes fly open. Her dad's not home yet. It must be her mom.

"Boo?" she says. "Can I come in?"

Violet sits up and straightens her hair. "Um ... sure."

Her mother enters her room, a Macy's shopping bag in her hand. She sits down beside Violet and puts the bag on the floor.

"How was your day?" she asks.

Inwardly, Violet shrinks. She hates these "How was your day?" sessions her mom has made a habit of. Nothing of value is ever shared, and afterward, Violet is left feeling more alone rather than less so. Violet has even had the traitorous thought that she misses her mother more now than she did when her mom was at the hospital. They just can't seem to connect.

"My day was fine," Violet says dully. "Yours?"

"Fun. Really fun," her mom says. She's more animated than usual, and it piques Violet's interest.

"How come?"

"Oh . . . because I went out and about, I guess. I went to that new mall, the street mall where music plays from hidden speakers and flowers bloom everywhere?"

Violet nods. "Thousand Oaks Village. It's nice."

"It is," Violet's mom agrees. Her skin has a sun-kissed warmth to it, and her eyes dance with amusement. "But those speakers. That piped in music. It's a bit . . . Disney, don't you think?"

"Yes!" Violet exclaims. She has thought that *exact same thing*. Her flower friends hear her out when she complains about it, but mainly they laugh and say, "It's just California." They *like* the artificial cheerfulness of it, maybe because it's all they're used to. They certainly don't understand why it creeps her out.

"It kind of creeped me out," her mom confides.

"Me, too!" Violet exclaims. "Because it's so . . . planned! Like the owners of the mall got together and thought, 'Now what can we do to lull these shoppers into a state of bliss, so that they will hand over all their money?'"

Her mom scoots closer to Violet. Violet scooches over to make room for her, so they can both lean against the headboard. Her mom kicks her shoes off and stretches her legs out alongside Violet's.

"Do you know what it reminded me of?" her mom asks. "*A Wrinkle in Time*, when Meg and Calvin and Charles Wallace reach the place where *It* lives."

Violet understands immediately. She and her mother read *A Wrinkle in Time* together when Violet was nine, and even though Violet was supposedly "too young" for it, she loved it. In the part her mother is referring to, the heroine of the book is trying to rescue her father, only everyone has been brainwashed into thinking the same exact way, doing things the same exact way, even bouncing balls the same exact way. The people in the town say they're happy, but it's clear to Meg that they no longer know what "happy" is. The only thing that matters, they think, is that everything looks clean and orderly on the outside. And if there *is* messiness, if a little boy bounces his ball to the wrong rhythm, for example, then he's whisked away and "retrained" until he can pass for perfect again.

"Did you notice how all the women look alike?" Violet says.

"*And* how they're all mainly women?" her mom replies.

"I think there are a lot of stay-at-home moms here," Violet says.

"Like me," Violet's mom says. "For a while, anyway."

This is the realest conversation Violet and her mom have had since her mom got home. Violet doesn't want to jeopardize things ... but there's a question she wants to ask, and yet is nervous about asking, and yet really *needs* to ask. *If* she wants things to keep being real.

She does, so she takes a breath and comes out with it. "Did being around all those pretty ladies who look alike, and the canned music, and the perfect potted plants ..."

Her mom takes Violet's hand, but she doesn't attempt to finish her sentence for her.

"Did it make you feel ... that bad way?" Violet says in a rush. In Atlanta, it was all the perfect stay-at-home moms that made Violet's mom have a breakdown, kind of. That's too easy of an explanation, but it's part of it.

"I can't," Violet remembers her mom saying, wilting on the kitchen floor of their old house. There was a charity ball to raise money for some cause or another, and according to Violet's mom, her hair was all wrong, her dress was all wrong, her perfume was all wrong, her lipstick was all wrong. Everything was all wrong, and she wilted like a fallen cake on the kitchen floor. And her parents didn't go to the charity ball, and Violet heard her dad call the babysitter, a girl named Tisha, and cancel on her.

Violet had been looking forward to hanging out with Tisha. They were going to make popcorn and watch *The Princess Diaries*, even though they'd both seen it tons of times already.

Violet's mom takes her time answering Violet's question. She traces Violet's long, slender fingers with her own. "Yes, Boo, it brings up the bad feelings."

Violet's lungs constrict.

"But not in the same way," Violet's mom says. "Because I can see them now. I can see them for what they are, and *I* can say yes or no to letting them in. And you know what?"

"What?"

"I didn't let them in. I said, 'Hello, bad feelings. And now, good-bye, bad feelings.'" Violet's mom smiles an open, uncomplicated smile. "And *then* do you know what

I did? I bought my daughter a fabulous new shirt, that's what."

"Really?" Violet says. "Let me see!"

Violet's mom leans over, grabs the Macy's bag, and lifts it onto the bed. She pulls the shirt out of the bag and shakes it out. It's white with a gothic-looking black cross on the front, but not in an emo-goth way.

Beneath the cross is a message: "Pave the path."

"It's beautiful," Violet murmurs. Back in Atlanta, her mom used to do this sort of thing often—surprise Violet with a new shirt or a cute skirt. All of that ended when she stopped leaving the house, of course. Still, Violet and her mom used to do lots of things, and have lots of good moments, and it's really nice to be reminded of that.

In Atlanta, before her mom got sick, Violet *was* happy. For the first time, Violet lets herself believe that happiness is possible here, in California, just as long as she's with her mom.

Her throat tightens, and she lets the message on her shirt seep in: *Pave the path.*

All she can do is try.

Friday, October 21

❈ Seventeen ❈

Katie-Rose

The class erupts in a cheer when Ms. Perez starts the day by announcing that due to a conflict, Mrs. Gundeck will not be one of the chaperones at the Lock-In tonight. As a result, she will be taking Mrs. Gundeck's place.

"Shhh!" Ms. Perez says, embarrassed and pleased. She glances at the door of her classroom to make sure Mrs. Gundeck isn't randomly strolling by, even though she's not even at school today due to her unanticipated conflict. "Kids, I'm happy I get to come, too. But we don't want to make Mrs. Gundeck feel bad, now do we?"

"We don't care!" Quin calls.

"You're not even going to the Lock-In," Katie-Rose points out, and Quin deflates a little. A shadow of regret passes over her face, and Katie-Rose thinks, *See, you big too-cool-for-school-er? You should just let yourself have FUN and not be Modessa's slave all the time.*

Katie-Rose isn't wasting her time on Quin, though. No way. She twists in her desk to check Preston's reaction, and he's grinning so widely (and un-meanly) that it throws her off. So she turns to Yaz, and the two girls give each other some knuckles, complete with the accompanying finger-burst explosion.

"You are so awesome," Yaz tells Katie-Rose. "*You* did this, you know."

Well, Preston did, Katie-Rose starts to say. But really, why confuse things? It was her idea after all. "Thanks. And *you* are even more awesome. Yesterday in trapeze class? Omigosh, you were like one of those Cirque du Soleil performers!"

Yasaman blushes.

Katie-Rose shoves her. "You were. Admit it. Out of everyone in the class, you were the only one who managed to do that ankle-dangling thing."

Yasaman bites her lower lip, then stops trying to be modest and beams. "I did, didn't I? And you will, too. Next time."

During morning break, Katie-Rose and Yaz find Milla and Violet so that they can all rejoice together.

"I am *sooo* excited about tonight!" Milla says, bouncing on the toes of her Skechers. "Pizza, junk food, movies—"

"*Max?*" Katie-Rose adds. "Cute little Max-Max?" She's still worried that her FFFs will get captured by maturity and bras and all of that, but she's decided to take a chill pill for tonight. Plus, she's decided that maybe (just maybe), there might be a place in the world for boys after all.

The only thing that dampens the girls' excitement is when Violet clears her throat and looks awkward and tells them that like Mrs. Gundeck, but for different reasons, she won't be coming to the Lock-In after all.

"Why?" Katie-Rose wails. "We need you! (a) For funness and (b) because our work is not yet done. Yes, Mr. Emerson and Ms. Perez will be jammed together AT NIGHTTIME, most likely in their NIGHTTIME ATTIRE—" She breaks off. "Do you think Ms. Perez will wear a nightie? One of those silky, sexy ones?"

"*No,*" Yaz says, hitting Katie-Rose. "And don't say that word. It's not appropriate."

"'Nightie' isn't appropriate?" Katie-Rose says.

Yasaman tilts her head and raises her eyebrows.

Katie-Rose shakes herself. "Whatever. Point is, we still have to get them to . . . make googly eyes at each other, or be alone in the teachers' lounge together, or something." She clasps her hands to her heart and gazes at the ceiling, heartbroken. "Otherwise they're just two lonely people who happen to be in the same place at the same time."

"Why can't you come?" Milla asks Violet. "I thought it was a done deal."

Violet's eyes shift to the left. She jerks her shoulders—a very un-Violet movement, as Violet is usually the epitome of self-control—and says, "Well . . . she, um . . . my *mom,* I mean . . . she changed her mind. She said I'm not allowed."

"Not allowed?" Yaz cries. "*Why?*"

Violet doesn't have a ready answer. Katie-Rose picks up on this, just as she picks up on the way color is rising in Violet's cheeks. Violet hardly *ever* blushes.

"She doesn't want me eating junk food that late in the night," Violet finally says.

"Bull pooty!" Katie-Rose says. Violet is hiding something. Either the real reason Violet's mom changed her mind is so incredibly mortifying that it can't be spoken aloud, or there *is* no real reason. Something fishy is going on, and Katie-Rose puts her hands on her hips.

"Isn't there any way you can persuade her to change her mind back?" Milla says. "It won't be nearly as fun without you, Violet."

"She's right," Yaz says. "It's supposed to be all four of us. The flower friends, all together."

"Listen, I'm sorry," Violet says. She won't meet their eyes.

"Are you sure you can't talk to her and just...explain?" Milla says. "She wants you to have fun, doesn't she?"

"Maybe the bigger question is do *you* want to have fun?" Katie-Rose says. "Because I feel like you're not fighting very hard for this."

Violet's temper flares. "Thanks. Thanks for making me feel better, y'all." She turns and flounces across the playground, and she doesn't come back.

Katie-Rose, Yaz, and Milla regard each other.

"I don't get it," Milla says.

"Yeah, something's not right," Yaz says.

Katie-Rose is put out. All this hard work, and now Violet isn't even going to be there? She flops back on the metal bench they're sitting on. "She needs to just … make it happen," she says.

Milla furrows her brow. Of the three girls, she is the most pensive. "I think … well, I don't know what I think. But what if she's lying? Or, not lying, but not exactly telling the truth?"

Katie-Rose lifts her eyebrows. "Meaning … ?"

"Maybe she's scared. Maybe it wasn't her mom who said she couldn't go."

"You think it's her dad?" Katie-Rose says incredulously. "Uh, no. I don't think so."

Milla shakes her head. "No, that's not what I mean."

"What, then?" Katie-Rose demands.

"Maybe she's still worried about leaving her mom alone," Yaz says. "Is that what you're thinking?"

Milla pauses, then nods.

"Well, that's just stupid!" Katie-Rose cries.

Yaz puts her hand on Katie-Rose's shoulder. "True," she says softly. "But sometimes people are."

Eighteen

Camilla

It's time! Time to decide (officially) what to wear to the Lock-In. Time to fix her hair, brush her teeth, and put on the teeniest bit of lip gloss. But first, time to turn on some really good music and turn it up LOUD, so she can flail about spastically and do jumping jacks and jog in place to get some, if not all, of her nervousness out. Dance therapy, this is called. Mom Abigail made it up. Usually it's for in the car, like back in the days when Milla hung out with Modessa and Quin and she never knew what cruel trick they might do, or tell *her* to do, and so she'd get a nervous tummy on the drive to school.

Mom Abigail would sense Milla's anxiety and crank the volume on the iPod dock.

"Let it out, baby," Mom Abigail would say. "Just let it out." And Mom Abigail would dance with her, to the extent that you can dance in a minivan. They'd bounce and shake wildly, and Milla would thrash her head so that her long blond hair whipped about, and it made things better. It did. Other drivers would give them the strangest looks, and Mom Abigail and Milla would fall into laughing fits, imagining how they must appear. The laughing, the frantic thrashing, the music . . . it let out some of the pressure which had built up inside of Milla, just as squeezing the plastic valve on a beach ball lets the air out.

Milla dances. She swishes her hair back and forth so that it hits her face. She *does* jog in place, super fast until she can hardly breathe, and then she throws herself flat on her back on her bed.

She pants, flinging her arms wide. She's happy under her layer of jitters, and she feels so lucky, so *blessed*, that she closes her eyes and tells God so with her heart. *Thank you*, she says silently. *For my friends, for my parents, for*

Max. For my body that can dance and my hair that can swish and my mouth that can smile.

Mom Abigail tells Milla that praying is important because praying lets you connect with God, and also with yourself. She also says that Milla can pray whenever and wherever she wants. Mom Abigail isn't obsessed with God, or with praying, but she does talk to Milla about stuff like that every so often. Also, Mom Abigail is the parent who takes Milla to church, while Mom Joyce has her own time with God by going for a bike ride or something like that. Mom Abigail doesn't mind that Mom Joyce doesn't come with them, because she says God is everywhere and everything.

"I just want church to be part of your life while you're young, so that you can decide for yourself if you want to go to church when you're a grown-up," she says. "More than that, I just want you to know how much God loves you."

"How much *does* God love me?" Milla says when they fall into these conversations. She knows what her mom will say. She just likes hearing it.

"Well, you know how much Mom Joyce and I love you,

right, pumpkin?" Mom Abigail will say, tilting up Milla's chin with her finger. "*That's* how much God loves you, and that is a lot. More than all the oceans in the world poured together. And for the record, God isn't some distant scowling old guy in the sky, either. God is just … *love*, that's how I see it."

Then Mom Abigail will go off on a tangent about how she doesn't want Milla thinking of God as someone who's watching her with hawk eyes to see if she does something wrong. She wants Milla to think of God as someone or something who knows Milla deeply and will always *always* love her, no matter what.

"Like Grandmommy?" Milla once asked, way back when she was little. Mom Abigail had laughed. "Yeah. Like Grandmommy."

That's why, when Milla prays, she tries to *feel* each word and thought that she sends out of herself. She wants God-Who-Is-Like-Grandmommy to know she means it.

When she's done with her thank-yous, she asks for God's guidance about an idea she has for helping Violet. Because she wasn't able to help Elena, and her failure makes her heart hurt. Her heart hurts for Elena *and* for herself, her old Elena-like self. She wonders if Elena feels sad, too—and that makes her feel even sadder.

But. Even though she failed to help Elena, that doesn't mean she should stop trying to help other people, does it? No way.

Um, so please help me help Violet, she prays. Then she opens her eyes. It's time to get ready.

Her nervousness feels more like a giddy, thrumming hum now. As she puts on her pink pj's, she thinks about Violet, because praying about something doesn't mean it's a done deal. Praying about something is a start, but Milla has to keep things going from here.

So, what does Milla know? She knows that Violet wants to come to the Lock-In, or did at one point. Violet was as excited as the others when the teachers first announced it. She also knows, or is pretty sure she knows, that Violet wasn't telling the truth when she told the flower friends that her mom had a sudden change of heart and said, "*NO, Violet, you may not go.* You have to stay home while all your other friends are out having fun."

It was Violet's body language when she told the girls she wouldn't be there tonight that makes Milla feel this way. Violet, in her normal state, is confident. She looks people in the eye. She doesn't hunch her shoulders and twist one foot behind the other.

Milla puts her hair in a high ponytail, wanting to look casual, but cute, too. She feels good about herself tonight . . . which is another blessing, as that's not always the case. Again she wishes that Violet felt good about herself, or good about life or her mom or whatever. When people feel good about themselves, they don't make up excuses for staying home on a party night.

She remembers a fragment of last week's Sunday school lesson, the day she drew a picture of her friends and her, only she made herself way shorter than the others. Today—this whole week, maybe—Violet has been feeling shorter than usual, Milla senses. Maybe that's a silly way to put it, and Milla knows Violet well enough to know that she'll sort things out eventually, but having her mom come home *has* to have been hard, no matter how positive Violet has made the situation out to be.

If plain old life can make Milla feel small and unsure of herself, doesn't it stand to reason that an event like having your mom come home from the hospital could make anybody feel small and uncertain? Even a girl as tall and strong and amazing as Violet? Like Alice falling down the rabbit hole, Milla thinks, and having everything go topsy-turvy. Growing huge, then small. Huge, then small.

Her Sunday school teacher's advice was to love your-self, and then pass that love on to someone else, and with a burst of resolve, that's what Milla decides to do.

"Milla?" her Mom Joyce calls. "Ready to roll?"

"One sec!" Milla calls back.

"'Kay, I'll be in the car!"

Milla doesn't have a phone in her own room, so she sticks her feet in her adorable bunny slippers and pads downstairs. Mom Abigail is off with friends, so Milla is able to use the kitchen phone in privacy.

She dials Violet's number, hoping that anyone other than Violet picks up. If Violet does answer, she'll go from there, but the person Milla really wants to talk to—*eek!*—is Violet's mom.

Her wish is granted. After two rings, a female voice—old, not kid-age—says, "Hello?"

"Um, is this Mrs. Truitt?" Milla asks.

"Yes. Who's this?"

"My name's Camilla. I'm one of Violet's friends."

"Oh, how lovely!" Mrs. Truitt says warmly. "Hold on and I'll get her for you."

"No, wait!" Milla says. Her palms are sweaty, but too bad. "I was actually, um, hoping to talk to you? If you have a minute?"

"To *me*?" Mrs. Truitt says. She sounds surprised, but not . . . weird or anything. "Ah . . . certainly. I don't see why not. What can I help you with?"

yasaman

The Lock-In is crazy . . . in a good way. Kids are hyper, everyone's bouncing off the walls, and Mr. Emerson and Ms. Perez don't even seem to care. They're standing together in the commons, chatting and laughing and curbing the kids' enthusiasm only when they have to, like when Preston—yes, Preston—tries to climb a bookshelf in order to retrieve a marble Chance inexplicably threw at the ceiling.

"Whoa there, buddy," Mr. Emerson calls to Preston. "Off the bookshelf. No climbing on the furniture, all right?"

"Yeah, *Preston*," Katie-Rose taunts, grinning. Yaz

knows that Katie-Rose didn't expect to see Preston here. She mentioned something to Yaz about how he thought The Lock-In was babyish, and how he would never waste his Friday night at a school activity.

Obviously, she was wrong.

Sitting side by side in the corner of the commons are Milla and Max. Yasaman's heart melts at the sight of them, they are just that adorable. Milla's pink pj's say "Peace, Love, and Turtles" across the front, and her bunny slippers have long ears that droop almost to the floor. Max is wearing the strangest pajamas Yaz has ever seen. They're pale blue and decorated with a variety of bizarre creatures: a brown octopus-slash-bat saying, "Hugs!"; a red robot with claw hands saying, "Boom! Beep!"; a piece of bacon saying, "I'm bacon!"; a sickly green zombie wearing a tie, lurching forward and saying, "Mmm! Brains!"

They're very geeky, but then, so is Max. He's showing Milla something on his iPhone, and since it's not technically school, Mr. Emerson and Ms. Perez don't seem to care. Max and Milla's heads are together, and they're both smiling, and that makes Yaz smile. Mr. Emerson leans closer to Ms. Perez and says something that makes her laugh out loud and then clap her hand over her mouth, and *that* makes Yaz's smile grow broader. She tries to edge up near enough to eavesdrop on her two adorable teachers, but there's too much wildness going on, with kids running amok and tackling each other—and tickling each other—and just all sorts of stuff.

But there is a spark between Mr. Emerson and Ms. Perez, and it's as bright as the spark between Max and Milla. Yasaman feels really, really proud of the flower friends for managing to get them some alone time, even if they're "alone" with a whole bunch of screaming kids.

Katie-Rose sneakily steals Preston's pizza from his paper plate, which he abandoned when he went to climb the bookshelf. She takes an impressively big bite and ambles over to Yasaman, her eyes bright. She's wearing her oversized CHICKS DON'T DIG STINKS shirt again (as a nightshirt, Yasaman supposes), and underneath it, a pair of girl-style purple boxers. They're "girl-style" because the front part, which is meant to open up, is sewed shut. Katie-Rose pointed that out to Yaz right off the bat.

"No penis hole!" she proclaimed, and not in a whisper.

"Katie-Rose! Hush!" Yasaman said, scandalized.

"Oh pooey on youey," Katie-Rose said. "You did that ankle drop move on the trapeze. I think you can handle the word *penis*."

Yasaman started to protest, then stopped. Katie-Rose did have a point.

With her big shirt, purple boxers, and her hair up in its usual high pigtails, Katie-Rose could almost be one of the strange creatures on Max's pajamas, if she were a cartoon instead of a girl.

"So what's cookin', good lookin'?" Katie-Rose says through a mouthful of cheese and pepperoni.

"Nothing much," Yasaman says.

"Well, that's because you're just *standing* there. Why are you just standing there?"

There was a time when Yasaman would have felt bad about herself for being the "just standing there" girl. That was before she grew wings. Now that she knows she doesn't *have* to just stand here, she realizes that she *can* just stand here, and that's fine.

Yasaman can be a watcher *and* a doer. Yasaman can be a well-behaved, modest Muslim girl *and* hang upside-down from a trapeze. Next week, Josie wants Yaz to work on doing more with the ropes. She thinks Yaz can master an intermediate level skill where she starts on the bar, grabs the ropes with her hands, and tucks into a ball, leaning backward and pulling her knees to her chest and her bottom off the bar. Then, with control, she'll straighten her body so that her feet are pointing up and her head is hanging below the bar, all the while keeping herself from falling just by holding on tight to the ropes.

"It requires a lot of core strength," Josie told Yasaman, pulling her to the side as the others chatted and gathered their stuff. "You're strong, though, and you're flexible. You're pretty much a natural, which is, like, *awesome*. As long as you're up for trying some moves that might feel freaky at first, I bet we can have you performing some advanced tricks by the end of the class. Wouldn't that rock?"

Yasaman felt the familiar flutterings of fear, but she didn't let that stop her. Instead, she told herself she simply had butterflies in her stomach, and what of it? She liked butterflies. She related to butterflies.

"So what do you say?" Josie asked. "You up for taking a leap of faith?"

Yasaman envisioned the yellow and orange butter-flies that flocked around her butterfly bush. She threw back her shoulders and told Josie, "Yes."

But Katie-Rose knows nothing of Yasaman's inner butterfly, because Yasaman didn't tell her. Some things she chooses to keep to herself. So as Katie-Rose elaborates on what a lump Yasaman is, Yasaman smiles and nods. She spots someone coming up behind them, someone of the boy persuasion, and grins slyly.

"Well, if you say I'm a lump, I guess I'm a lump," Yaz says. "What about you, Katie-Rose? Looks like you're hav-ing fun with Preston, hmm?"

"What?!" Katie-Rose exclaims. "*No!*" She takes another big bite of his pizza, and she is not ladylike about it at all. "Preston is annoying and obnoxious and should be put in the zoo."

Preston puts his mouth next to her ear. "In the Cool People area, or the monkey cage, with you?"

Katie-Rose squeals. She whips around and cries, "*Pres*ton!"

"Hey, hold on," Preston says, eyeing her pizza. He looks

over his shoulder at his empty paper plate, then back at the half-eaten slice in her hand. "Is that my pizza?!"

"No?"

"You stole my pizza!" Preston says.

"Possession is nine-tenths of the law!" she cries, dashing off. Preston chases her, Katie-Rose squeals some more, and Yasaman shakes her head.

Chicks *do* dig stinks, it seems. Or at least the stink-makers. And lumps transform into butterflies, and butterflies transform into girls named Yasaman.

No, wait, butterflies don't transform *into* Yasaman. Yasaman is a ten-year-old girl, and will stay a ten-year-old girl until she grows up. Yaz started off as a baby, not a caterpillar. But if someone was to suggest that Yasaman was transformed *by* butterflies, Yasaman wouldn't be afraid to examine the notion.

Yasaman is all about taking leaps of faith.

Twenty

Violet

The drive to Rivendell feels like a flashback from her past. Why?

- Because Violet and her parents used to drive home in the evenings from big family gatherings in Georgia. Dusk would have fallen, and the moon would be creeping up, and Violet would gaze out of her backseat window into the dark.

- Because Violet felt cozy in the back of the car, knowing her parents were up front. Listening to them talk softly about Granny Truitt's ham, which she soaked in Coca-Cola, and Aunt Joycie's corn casserole, which Violet's daddy could never get enough of, and poor Mary and Charles with Lucas, that no-good son of theirs, who might end up homeless and on the streets at the rate he was going.

- Because they were a family on those dark-outside drives. They were a unit, separated from the rest of the world by glass and metal and gentle conversation, and every so often, Violet's dad would laugh, and it would be a laugh of surprise and delight, because Violet's mom could do that. She could make him laugh like that, as few others ever did.

- Because Violet wasn't expected to participate in their discussions as her father navigated the windy Georgia hills. She wasn't forbidden to participate, or even discouraged from participating, but nothing was expected of her, *because she was the kid and they were the parents.*

As her parents drive her to Rivendell, those long-ago memories add a sense of déjà vu to *this* car ride, which is happening not in the past but in the present. As in *right now*. Yes, Violet is older, and the SUV is new since their trips to visit their Southern relatives. But her parents chat easily in the front of the car while Violet listens from the back, her forehead pressed to the cool window as she gazes into the dark.

It's a pocket of grace, because for the first time since her mom got home, Violet doesn't overanalyze things. She doesn't think, *If I do this, will Mom be sad? If I don't do this, will Mom be sad? If I'm careful and diligent and don't "upset the apple cart," to use a Granny Truitt expression, will Mom keep smiling like she did yesterday? If I keep my eyes open and stay vigilant, can I make sure she never feels that bad way again?*

She just sits in the back seat of the SUV in gray sweats and a soft white T-shirt, because sorry, that's all the Lock-In is getting from her in the way of pj's.

Yasaman will be wearing something proper. Most of her skin will be covered, and so will her hair. Katie-Rose will be wearing . . . oh, who knows? An elephant costume? A long lacy nightgown that she thinks is ironic? A pair of her brother's *Toy Story* pajamas?

As for Milla, she'll look adorable in some flavor of adorable girl pajamas. They'll be the sort of pajamas that are *meant* to be pajamas rather than ending up that way just because they're soft and comfy.

When Violet thinks about Milla . . . *hmm*. What sensations arise in her body? What does she feel? She feels a slight tightness around her ribs, because *Milla called her mom*. She told her all about the Lock-In, which Violet did at one point want to attend, only that was before she had such a good day with her mom yesterday. Maybe she changed her mind out of a superstitious fear that things could fall apart again if she wasn't there to hold them together.

So yeah, there was some anger at Milla for being a busybody, but Violet pretty much let it go when she saw how happy her mom was that Violet was going to a party, a real live party with friends and pizza and too much Coke.

"Why didn't you tell me, you silly?" her mom said after

getting off the phone with Milla. "I *want* you to have fun. If you don't, I'm not doing my job as your mother."

Violet had never thought about it like that.

"I've been worried about you," her mom continued. "When I was your age, I ran all over the place with my friends. But I haven't met a single one of your friends, Violet. Your father tells me you have friends, and that I need to give things time to readjust, but it's hard."

"I know," Violet said.

"Well . . . will I get to meet Camilla when we drop you off? She sounded very nice on the phone."

"Of course, Mom. My three best friends will all be there. If you want me to, I'll introduce you to all of them."

Her mother readily agreed, and when they pull into the Rivendell parking lot, she flips the mirror open on her visor and checks her lipstick.

"You look great," Violet's dad says.

"You smell good, too," Violet adds. *Fleur de la Fée,* the violet-scented perfume that smells like it's supposed to again, now that her mom's acting like *she's* supposed to again.

"I don't see many cars," Violet's mom muses. "I thought lots of kids were coming? I like the building, though. It looks like a very nice school."

"It is, and the other kids are probably already here. It started at six."

"At six?" Violet's mother cries. "But it's—"

"It's fine," Violet's dad says. "Violet will make a fashionable entrance. You can handle that, right, Violet?"

"Absolutely," Violet says. She's handled so many things this week, all of them harder than making a fashionable entrance.

She climbs out of the Range Rover. It's so high up, she has to jump to the ground. "You two coming?" she asks her parents.

"As long as you don't mind," Violet's mom says. "And as long as you're telling the truth when you say you don't mind."

"Come on," Violet says, linking her arm through her mother's.

They cross the parking lot, her father walking alongside them. They go up the stairs to Rivendell's front door.

It's locked, probably for safety reasons since it's a night-time event.

Violet's dad raps on the glass door, and Thomas glances over. He's walking on his hands. Who knows why? He tumbles to the floor and calls out, "Max!" That's what it looks like he says, anyway.

Violet and her parents are in the dark, and the Lock-In kids are inside, lit up like stars, and Violet has a moment of panic. She almost turns around. She almost decides this was a very, very bad idea.

Then she catches the swish of blond hair from over in the corner of the commons, and Milla is dashing over with Max right behind her. She pushes open the door, and *wham*. Sounds grow louder and lights grow brighter. There's lots of laughter and rowdy conversations. There are pajamas and pajamas and pajamas.

"Violet! You're here!" Milla exclaims. She throws herself at Violet and embraces her. Violet staggers, but keeps her balance.

Milla pulls back. To Violet's mother, she says, "And you're Violet's mom?"

"I am," she says. Her smile is as warm as Milla's.

"It's really nice to meet you," Milla says. She looks from Violet to her mom. "You two look alike. Do people always tell you that?"

"All the time," Violet and her mother say in unison.

Milla laughs. So do Violet and her mom.

"Two peas in a pod," Violet's dad says.

"Da-a-a-ad," Violet groans. In Atlanta, people *did* remark all the time about how much Violet and her mom resembled each other, and "two peas in a pod" was her dad's standard response.

This is the first time it's happened in California, though. Violet doesn't really mind her dad's comment. She's not mad at Milla anymore, either. Her anger just . . . *whish.* Went away.

Milla turns and calls, "Yaz! Katie-Rose! Get over here!"

Yasaman is already flying their way. Knowing Yaz, she noticed Violet's presence almost as soon as Milla did. As for Katie-Rose, she seems to be having a food fight with . . .

"Is that *Preston*?" Violet says.

"Uh-huh," Yasaman says, breathing slightly harder

than normal. Her *hijab* flutters over her shoulders. "Hi, Mrs. Truitt," she says, smiling shyly at Violet's mom. As polite as ever, she turns to Violet's dad and includes him as well. "Hi, Mr. Truitt."

Katie-Rose spots the group by the front door, and her eyes grow huge. She slaps a battered slice of pizza on Preston's chest, and it promptly falls off.

"Hey!" Preston complains, but Katie-Rose has abandoned him and is running over. There is pepperoni sauce in her hair. Violet looks closer. There is also an actual pepperoni in her hair.

"Mom, this is Katie-Rose," Violet says.

"You're Violet's mom?" Katie-Rose says. "Her real live mom, in the flesh and everything?"

"Oh good grief," Violet mutters, but her mom takes it in stride. It occurs to Violet that she needs to trust her mom more, and also that she probably shouldn't be surprised at how well Violet's mom is dealing with her friends, even over-the-top Katie-Rose. Katie-Rose is no manicured mall walker, that's for sure.

Holding out her arm, Violet's mom says, "Real and in the flesh. You can pinch me if you'd like."

Katie-Rose does, of course, because she's Katie-Rose. She leaves pizza sauce on Violet's mom's skin.

"Oopsy daisy," she says, her cheeks turning pink.

"No big deal," Violet says. She holds the doors open for her parents. "Come on in—we'll find a napkin and I can introduce both of y'all to some more people, like my teachers, for example."

Mr. Emerson and Ms. Perez are already heading their way, drawn by the commotion. Other kids glance over with interest. Natalia, Ava, Becca. Preston and Thomas and . . . *whoa*, Cyril Remkiwicz? Violet never would have expected to see Cyril here, but he sure seems happy, in his Eeyore way, to see her. She waves. He waves back.

"You have a lot of friends," Violet's mom comments.

I do, Violet marvels.

"Yep, she does," Yasaman announces. There's something different about Yaz, but Violet can't put her finger on it. It's something good, whatever it is. She'll figure it out eventually. Also, at some point, she needs to ask how the trapeze class went, for Yaz *and* Katie-Rose. Plus she wants to hear how things are progressing with Mr.

Emerson and Ms. Perez, and she can't forget to get the latest scoop on Max and Milla.

Oh, and Katie-Rose and Preston! Is there possibly a scoop developing between them? No? Yes? Maybe? Along the same lines, is it possible that any bottles have made guest appearances at this shindig, as in the spinning sort of bottles? If so, who spun them? Who was there when they *stopped* spinning and switched to pointing?

There's so much life going on all around her, and she almost missed it by staying home. She almost missed it, and not only that, but she almost made her mom miss it, too. Her mom's face is bright as she makes easy chitchat with Ms. Perez. Her dad is more reserved, but he's certainly friendly as he shakes Mr. Emerson's hand.

Milla's arm loops around Violet's waist, and Yasaman, who's on her other side, squeezes Violet's hand. Katie-Rose moves behind them and throws both arms around all three of them.

"Mmm-wah!" Katie-Rose says, planting a smooch on Milla's cheek. She angles in and kisses Violet and Yasaman as well. "And mmm-wah and mmm-wah!"

"Katie-Rose!" Milla says. Her hand goes to her cheek.

"Do I have pizza sauce on me? Did you pizza-sauce me, Katie-Rose?"

Yasaman giggles as she wipes off her cheek.

Violet soaks up the moment and commits it to memory, hugging her friends tight.

Saturday, October 22

❊ Twenty-One ❊

The Flower Box

MarshMilla:	omigosh, that was the BEST NIGHT EVER!!! I had sooooo much fun. I went to bed all zingy, and I woke up zingy, and I'm STILL zingy.
MarshMilla	are the rest of you zingy, too? 🙄
The*rose*Knows:	+zips wildly around bedroom+ +bounces on bed+ +scales walls and does backward flip off ceiling+
The*rose*Knows:	does that count as zingy? cuz if so, then yeah, I suppose one might say I'm feeling

a weensy bit of zing in my zing-a-ding-ding.

ultraviolet: um, 1st off, that just sounds wrong. your zing-a-ding-ding? and secondly, based on how hyper you were last night, I'd say you're more than a weensy bit zingy.

The*rose*Knows: okay, ya got me. I am ZINGILICIOUS, that's what I am! which is to say that yes, I had an absolutely fabulous time last night, and I wish there was another Lock-In tonight!
👍😜👍

MarshMilla: I saw u, u know. during that mirroring game Mr. Emerson invented, where everyone paired up and faced each other and had to do whatever their partner did?

Yasaman: oh my goodness, u and Preston were SO adorable. All I cld think was, "so much for being antiromance, huh, Katie-Rose?"

Yasaman: i can still see it: how YOU leaned in, and then HE leaned in . . .

MarshMilla: and then YOU closed your eyes, and HE closed HIS eyes . . .

ultraviolet: and then u freaked out and jumped back like someone had poured red-hot fire ants down your PJ bottoms. 😂

Yasaman: hee hee, that *was* pretty funny.

The*rose*Knows: that's enuff, you guys +gives FFFs the hairy eyeball+

MarshMilla: did u suddenly realize what was about to happen? that you and preston were going to KISS?

The*rose*Knows: +gives FFFs VERY SCARY HAIRY EYEBALL+ 😠

The*rose*Knows: I said shut it!!!

ultraviolet: u shld have gone for it, k-r

Yasaman: smoochie-smoochie! 😚

The*rose*Knows: omigosh.

The*rose*Knows: You. Are going. To stop. TALKING ABOUT PRESTON NOW. 'kay? raise yr hand if u understand.

ultraviolet: can't. too busy typing,

MarshMilla:	yeah, what she said. and I can't stop giggling, either. sorry!!!
Yasaman:	Katie-Rose, even u have to admit it's funny. I mean, *all* week long u pooh-poohed everything lovey-dovey, and then tonight came, and 3 hours, 2 slices of pizza, and 1 mirror game later—BLAM! *everything* changed!
ultraviolet:	so true. out of the four of us, I always thought Milla wld be the first to kiss a boy.
MarshMilla:	Violet!
MarshMilla:	😶😶😶
Yasaman:	now Milla, u know how cute u & Max are. I'll prolly never have a boyfriend—and I'm not READY for a boyfriend, and anyway my dad wld kill me and my imaginary boyfriend— but for you two, it's super fab.
ultraviolet:	I agree, and I'd like to add that it's 100% super fab that Preston, aka Fart King, has a major crush on Katie-Rose.
The*rose*Knows:	he does not!
MarshMilla:	oh, plz. then why did he smear pizza all

over you? and later on, why did you two have that pillow fight, hmm?

ultraviolet: not just a pillow fight, but a pillow fight involving multiple pink Pillow Pals in the shape of unicorns.

Yasaman: yeah. u better be glad Nigar wasn't there, cuz one of those pillow pals was hers.

The*rose*Knows: listen, the pillow pals were just sitting there in the preschoolers' cubbies. If the preschoolers didn't want us . . . liberating them . . . then they shld have taken them home over the weekend.

Yasaman: only they're not allowed to. they keep them at school for the whole year, for nap time.

The*rose*Knows: details, details. anyhoodle, no pink unicorns were harmed in our pillow pal fight, so it wldn't hold up in a court of law.

MarshMilla: moving on!

MarshMilla: speaking of superfab couples, didn't you think Mr. E and Ms. P seemed to really like each other?

ultraviolet: MY MOM assumed they were a couple. when

I took her over to meet them, they were both, like, glowing. they chatted with my mom and dad, and everyone was all smiles.

ultraviolet: then, after the Lock-In ended, my mom asked if Mr. Emerson and Ms. Perez were "an item."

Yasaman: see? they have good chemistry!

MarshMilla: I saw Mr. Emerson brush his fingertips over Ms. Perez's hand.

ultraviolet: U did?!

MarshMilla: he even gave her hand a quick squeeze. I'm not even kidding.

Yasaman: oh my goodness, this is so exciting!!!!!!

Yasaman:

The*rose*Knows: well, *I* heard them arguing. They were handing out pizza, and I went back for seconds, and it was NOT all rainbows and ponies. It sounded like they were having a fight.

MarshMilla: a *fight?* about what?

The*rose*Knows: well . . . about the thing they were fighting about. that's what.

ultraviolet: which wld be . . . ?

The*rose*Knows: they were arguing about food, all

                 right?

Yasaman: **food? Why wld they argue about food?**

MarshMilla: explain more

The*rose*Knows: well, Mills, they liked yr brownie. that's the

                 first thing I overheard.

MarshMilla: that doesn't sound like a fight. that

                 sounds like an un-fight.

The*rose*Knows: but then they started talking about

                 desserts in general, which apparently

                 they both like.

Yasaman: **we knew that already. liking homemade**

                 baked goods is one of the things they have

                 in common!

The*rose*Knows: but u haven't heard the bad part yet, and

                 the bad part is . . . +cue scary music+ . . .

                 coconut

ultraviolet: COCONUT?

The*rose*Knows: so innocent, so deadly

The*rose*Knows: and so sad that all yr hard work—I mean

                 all OUR hard work—ended up cracked

to pieces by the humble, strangely furry coconut. 🥥

ultraviolet:	does anyone know what she's talking about?
MarshMilla:	well, Mr. Emerson doesn't like coconut. he told us that in class.
Yasaman:	so . . . what? Ms. Perez *does* like coconut?
The*rose*Knows:	that's the impression I got, prolly cuz she said, and I quote, "Coconut is delicious! What are you talking about, you crazy man?" and then she swatted him.
MarshMilla:	oh good grief. that is called FLIRTING, you doof!
Yasaman:	oh, yay! I didn't *think* coconut wld be a deal breaker!
The*rose*Knows:	whatevah.
MarshMilla:	Project Teacherly Lurve worked, peeps! we did it!!!!
MarshMilla:	and that includes u, katie-rose, despite yr grumpy-lumpiness. 🧁
MarshMila:	that's a coconut-flavored cupcake, btw. with flies.
The*rose*Knows:	💩

The*rose*Knows: that's a poop, btw. with stink lines coming up from it.

MarshMilla: there was *one* sad thing last night, tho.

Yasaman: **what?**

MarshMilla: max and I were looking at the bulletin board by the front door—the one with photos of Rivendell kids and teachers thumbtacked all over it? and smack in the middle was a picture from our Snack Attack assembly last month. It was of elena and her pig, porkchop.

Yasaman: 😟

MarshMilla: I know. They both looked so happy in that picture.

The*rose*Knows: and now Elena is evil chick #3

MarshMilla: but she doesn't really *want* to be an evil chick. I know she doesn't, because when I was under modessa's spell, I didn't want to be evil, either.

MarshMilla: I think we need to help her.

ultraviolet: how? you already tried, and you failed. plus, doesn't Elena get to be in charge of her own

life? if we barge in and try to interfere . . .
well, how is that different than when Katie-
Rose interfered by signing me and Yaz up
for trapeze lessons?

The*rose*Knows: heyyyy!

MarshMilla: yeah, but it worked out! yaz, aren't u
glad katie-rose stepped in and
interfered?

Yasaman: Um, I'm glad I'm in the class, and I wouldn't
be if not for Katie-Rose. So I guess so.

The*rose*Knows: if you're trying to say thank you, ur
welcome.

Yasaman: On the other hand, interfering in ppl's lives
is . . . oh, I don't know. Complicated? Not
always the right thing to do?

MarshMilla: but when it IS the right thing to do, we
should do it, right? flowers for justice?
flowers who believe in making the world
a better place???

The*rose*Knows: ohhhh. u want Elena to be our next
project, don't you?

MarshMilla: not like that. not like she's our project,

like we're going to give her a makeover
and turn her into a different person. but
yes, I do think we shld get her away from
modessa and quin.

Yasaman:	but how?
ultraviolet:	Yaz has a point. but you're a really nice person to *want* to help her, mills.
The*rose*Knows:	blah blah blah
Yasaman:	I have another idea . . .
The*rose*Knows:	tell us
Yasaman:	well, Nigar's b-day is November 18th. She'll be 4! Can you believe it? She wants to have a "bubblegum party," whatever that means. I was hoping maybe we could be party helpers together. Do you want to?
The*rose*Knows:	yes yes yes! I am awesome at parties!
ultraviolet:	a bubblegum party? we could make up bubblegum games, I guess.
MarshMilla:	like pin the tail on the bubble?
The*rose*Knows:	POP!
ultraviolet:	ok, maybe not pin the tail on the bubble, but we're smart. I bet we can come up with

all sorts of bubblicious ideas once we put our minds to it.

Yasaman: **so you'll do it? you'll help?**

MarshMilla: Of course. I love nigar. And will the three of you promise to think about helping elena, too? and to think HARD about it?

Yasaman: **yes**

Ultraviolet: 😉

The*rose*Knows: fine, fine. sheesh.

MarshMilla: oh, yay. Flower Power Forever!!!!!!!!!!

Acknowledgments

Butterfly kisses galore to the usual crew. You make my heart sing; you give my imagination wings. Thank you . . . and you and you and you. You know who you are.

About the Author

Lauren Myracle *really* likes tweens and pre-tweens; she'd rather sit at the kids' table than at the boring grown-up table any day. She's written squillions of books, including the bestselling Internet Girls series and the Winnie Years series, and she is SO SUPER EXCITED about the Flower Power series. Why? Because at last she's written books that blend the thrills of social media with the goofy, wonderful madness of fifth grade.

Visit her on the web at laurenmyracle.com, and come hang with Milla, Violet, Yasaman, and Katie-Rose at flowerpowerbooks.info.